I0709078

A TASTE FOR A MATE

A REDWOOD PACK NOVEL

CARRIE ANN RYAN

A Taste for a Mate
A Redwood Pack Novel
By: Carrie Ann Ryan
© 2012 Carrie Ann Ryan
Ebook ISBN: 978-1-62322-001-3
Print ISBN: 978-1-943123-22-3
Cover Art by Charity Hendry

This ebook is licensed for your personal enjoyment only. This ebook may not be re-sold or given away to other people. If you would like to share this book with another person, please purchase an additional copy for each person or use proper retail channels to lend a copy. If you're reading this book and did not purchase it, or it was not purchased for your use only, then please return it and purchase your own copy. Thank you for respecting the hard work of this author.
All characters in this book are fiction and figments of the author's imagination.

A TASTE FOR A MATE

A Redwood Pack Novel

By

Carrie Ann Ryan

PRAISE FOR CARRIE ANN RYAN

"One of the best family romance series around! Carrie Ann Ryan brings the heat, emotions, and love in each story!" ~ NYT Bestselling Author Corinne Michaels

"Count on Carrie Ann Ryan for emotional, sexy, character driven stories that capture your heart!" – Carly Phillips, NY Times bestselling author

"Carrie Ann Ryan's romances are my newest addiction! The emotion in her books captures me from the very beginning. The hope and healing hold me close until the end. These love stories will simply sweep you away." ~ NYT Bestselling Author Deveny Perry

"Carrie Ann Ryan writes the perfect balance of sweet and heat ensuring every story feeds the soul." - Audrey Carlan, #1 New York Times Bestselling Author

"Carrie Ann Ryan never fails to draw readers in with passion, raw sensuality, and characters that pop off the page. Any book by Carrie Ann is an absolute treat." – New York Times Bestselling Author J. Kenner

"Carrie Ann Ryan knows how to pull your heartstrings and make your pulse pound! Her wonderful Redwood Pack series will draw you in and keep you reading long into the night. I can't wait to see what comes next with the new generation, the Talons. Keep them coming, Carrie Ann!" –

Lara Adrian, New York Times bestselling author of CRAVE THE NIGHT

"With snarky humor, sizzling love scenes, and brilliant, imaginative worldbuilding, The Dante's Circle series reads as if Carrie Ann Ryan peeked at my personal wish list!" – NYT Bestselling Author, Larissa Ione

"Carrie Ann Ryan writes sexy shifters in a world full of passionate happily-ever-afters." – *New York Times* Bestselling Author Vivian Arend

"Carrie Ann's books are sexy with characters you can't help but love from page one. They are heat and heart blended to perfection." *New York Times* Bestselling Author Jayne Rylon

Carrie Ann Ryan's books are wickedly funny and deliciously hot, with plenty of twists to keep you guessing. They'll keep you up all night!" USA Today Bestselling Author Cari Quinn

"Once again, Carrie Ann Ryan knocks the Dante's Circle series out of the park. The queen of hot, sexy, enthralling paranormal romance, Carrie Ann is an author not to miss!" *New York Times* bestselling Author Marie Harte

A TASTE FOR A MATE

Jasper Jameson has spent his life caring for others, knowing that one day he might be blessed with his mate. He's fought alongside his family and Pack for over a century but it isn't until he meets a human who makes his wolf growl, that he knows that there's something more than fate worth fighting for.

When Jasper walks into Willow Delton's bakery she knows there's something different about him. But every time he walks back out again, she doesn't know what to think. When he finally finds the strength to ask her out, a new enemy in Jasper's life has other plans.

A dangerous Pack is on the prowl and they've not only threatened the Redwood Pack but brought a demon into the fold as well. Forced into a new way of life, Jasper and

Willow must fight not only for their lives but their weakening mating bond. Trust takes time but the two of them might not have as much as they need.

PROLOGUE

Smells of sulfur and ash permeated the Circle as the rhythmic beating of drums mixed with growls and murmurs. Voices elevated as Taiko drums increased in tempo, matching the heartbeats of the Pack around Corbin.

A blond male in low-slung jeans howled as he eyed the bare breasts of the woman next to him. The man beside him gave a sharp growl while beating his chest. Corbin stood outside the mass of people and felt the rising tension creep up his arms. *Nice.*

Corbin was the Alpha's only son and Heir. His people shouted for him, begging for his presence. The Pack must make a sacrifice, but he would rather play with his new project. His last one endured only a few short days. What a waste of soft flesh.

A scream ripped from the throat of a young woman

behind him. Corbin inhaled her fear and smiled. The sickly, metallic taste felt heavy on his tongue. An aphrodisiac for a wolf like him. Flesh slapping flesh in painful bursts silenced her. Corbin tilted his head toward the crowd and it parted. Their rumblings of conversation quieted as their Alpha's presence commanded their upmost attention.

Following his father, Corbin entered the Circle, not bothering to look at whom he passed. These lowlifes of the Pack meant nothing to him. He stopped beside his father in the center and looked around. They were manic with frantic energy, eager to see the outcome of their sacrifice. He lifted his chin to signal the entrance of their main entertainment.

Four men walked from between groups of boulders, carrying two wooden planks. Chains circled the flat boards to encase two young, frightened women. The pale haired one made no sound and remained unmoving, her eyes wide and vacant. The other, this one with raven hair, struggled, moaned, then screamed for freedom. The men dropped their captives in an inelegant heap. But really, these girls didn't deserve much more.

He looked down at the dark-haired one who continued to fight her bonds. How dare this bitch have the audacity to fight? Didn't she know it was useless? Fighting only showed her disregard for her betters – for him. Corbin's hand came down across her face. His sharp strike reverberated through the air. But as he raised his fist to permanently shut her up, his father called him.

"No, Corbin, let your sister be for now. For her regrettable uselessness and her inability to submit, she will be the demon's bribe to do with as he wishes." His father curled his lip and snorted before he quickly masked his features.

The slut deserved what she got.

Gesturing to the other woman, who had long since given in to her fate, his father spat on the ground. "Your cousin, on the other hand, will do what is needed. Like a good bitch. She will be sacrificed first for the calling."

Raising his fist, he yelled to his Pack. The answering call vibrated through the forest, and the steady beat of the drums intensified.

The Pack's desire to conquer crawled along Corbin's skin, tickling his nerves. Inhaling, he savored it. *Ah, it's almost time.*

Walking toward him, his father spoke again. "You still have one sister left once this is done, and you'll still have your plaything." He growled a laugh as Corbin turned his head to the right and looked into the field past the group of his followers at his younger sister.

Ellie's brown hair lay lank on her shoulders and dirt smudges adorned her face, her bloodied lip only now healing from his earlier play. She could have been so much more, been by his side in a position of power. But alas, she didn't share his views. Unmoving, she watched the proceeding with a fire in her eyes that belied her submission. She would not be easily quieted, and Corbin relished it.

"Use this." His father handed him a silver dagger with red rubies on its hilt. "It's been bespelled by a witch and only needs the blood of a living sacrifice to tear the veil and bring forth our demon."

Corbin smiled and took the blade, running his finger along the sharp edge, careful not to cut himself and destroy the magic. He looked down at his captives on their boards and smiled. *Oh, this will be fun.*

Corbin brushed the pale hair out of his cousin's eyes before bending down over her bruised face to whisper in her ear. "You will be a good girl now and accept your honor. Through you, we will finally conquer the Redwood Pack. You are doing us a service; remember that."

A final whimper left her swollen lips before he straightened to his full height and plunged the dagger into her chest. No sound escaped as the frail light in her eyes faded to darkness.

"Take our bounty, our blood. We give freely, this magic of death. Sacrifice meets endless faith. Cross the veil. Meet your summoners."

His father's voice echoed through the forest again as the blood of Corbin's cousin drenched the dirt floor of their sacred Circle nestled in the forest. Lightning arched across the cloudless sky, and fire erupted in a ring, surrounding the Pack. Growls and yells grew louder as the smell of death and sulfur increased. The dark scents of ash and sulfur seeped into his pores. Invigorating. The thumping energy of the dark magic mingled with the loud resonance of the drums, as a flash of bright lighting scattered across the tree line causing the Pack to jump.

The drums stopped and voices hushed as a lone man appeared through a gap in the bodies. Not a man – no. Dressed in a fine black suit, he was dangerously beautiful with a face smooth like granite. Only the red irises of his eyes gave away the fact he was not of this world. No, not man, but a demon. Their demon.

CAYM TOOK clean and precise steps into the Circle from the forest where he'd broken through the veil between Earth and Hell, and arched a brow at their offerings. The Alpha's daughter was indeed a fine specimen and a decent bounty. But he wouldn't have expected anything less. If this Pack wanted his power to aid in their quest, true sacrifice was the only option. The eager faces of the Pack stared at him with need. Their scent of tension and anticipation washed over him. Yes, this Pack would do. His lips quirked into a smile.

Ah werewolves, still lower class and ill-bred. Caym would enjoy killing this raven-haired wolf before he killed his way through the others. Walking through the veil on the tails of death released him into this world. He'd be forced into aiding this Pack – but he would have his freedom and taste the blood he so desired.

"Demon!" A tall man with caramel skin and dark hair bellowed. Power radiated off him in waves.

Ah, the Alpha of the little wolf Pack.

"We call on you to aid us in our time of need to destroy the Redwood Pack and claim our rightful, dominant place," the other man continued, and Caym fought the urge to roll his eyes. "We offer you the most prized female as your bounty. Do with her as you wish."

The Alpha's arrogant face could not hide the blatant fear in his eyes. Yes, he was wise to be fearful of him; after all, demons were relegated to Hell for a reason. And Caym was among the worst.

Struggling against her chains, her bronzed flesh bloodied and bruised, the dark-haired female enticed him. He smiled.

With a nod at the Alpha and the werewolf beside him, Caym strolled toward his gift. He traced his finger down her cheek, loving the feel of her blood pulsating against his skin. She jerked way from his touch, so he pressed harder.

He loved it when they fought.

He trailed his fingers down, resting them on her breasts. Her eyes widened before he dug his claws into her flesh to feel the beat of her heart. Her blood pooled around his hand, the warmth spreading along his cool skin. Delicious.

The girl's final scream set his blood to boil and filled his cock.

Holding her warm beating heart above her now lifeless form, he smiled. Caym lifted it over his head before letting out a mighty roar.

Death by his hands. The sweetest of sacrifices.

"A deal with the Devil indeed." Caym spoke clearly, eager to find his next victim, no matter where it came from. "I accept." He gave his best, almost civilized, smile. If his cruelty showed through it, how was he to blame? He'd tried.

1

———

The scent of cinnamon and sugar danced on the air as Willow Delton heaved opened the heavy oven door to remove her prized cinnamon rolls. The plump, buttery pastries were baked to perfection, and she set them on the counter to cool. The only thing missing was her thick and creamy frosting, but that would have to wait.

Willow stood back and stared around her commercial grade kitchen. She'd started her bakery from scratch, and it had grown into a successful, albeit small, business. Incredible, really. She'd never thought the day would arrive when she finally had a place to call her own. She was right where she wanted to be. Her favorite part of the day was being able to meet one-on-one with her customers. She loved the looks on their faces when they bit into her temptations, that look of ecstasy not seen on this side of the bedroom door that flashed across their eyes.

Of course, that particular look as the result of a man was long absent from Willow's face. Too excruciatingly long.

She stood back and closed her eyes, conjuring the memory of her mystery man's face. The image that filled her mind made her forget the lack of human contact. The thought of his deep, husky voice tickled her spine whenever he spoke. Green eyes caught her in his web with only a glance. She'd fallen for a stranger and didn't even know his name. He'd come into her store every morning and ordered a cinnamon roll and coffee with only a few words. Then he 'd pay cash before lifting up the corner of his mouth in a semblance of a smile and walking out of her store. Was it strange she worried he'd keep walking and never return?

A bell's tinkle pulled Willow from her reverie and self-pity. As she turned to greet her customer, her heart leapt to her throat. Him. Her mysterious fantasy man. As she tried to regain her senses, she took all of him in. He had to be one of the tallest men she'd ever seen, easily over six and a half feet. The tight black T-shirt he wore hugged his biceps and cut into his muscular physique, while his broad shoulders stretched and strained the seams. His body tapered down to a narrow waist and hips as they met his thighs. His long legs she wanted to grip, encased in worn jeans lead to work boots. Hmm, construction perhaps? She glanced back up his body to his striking face.

He wasn't beautiful, but he did have a face most women would dream about. A strong jaw and cheekbones gave him an aura of strength, the kind of strength that would be protective. His hair was midnight black and long enough to brush his shoulders, however, today, a band held it back, showcasing his face more. He studied her, his green eyes calm and calculating. Willow let out a surprised gasp at the sexual heat radiating from him. Could she possibly be imagining things?

JASPER JAMENSON FOUGHT himself as he walked into the bakery that morning. This would be the seventh week in a row he'd come here, every day but Sunday. And that was only because the damn store was closed. As good as the cinnamon rolls were, and they were little tastes of heaven, it was the woman behind the counter that brought him there every morning.

Following a particularly bad night in the forest on a hunt, Jasper had been pissed and hungry. Another wolf had tried to play a dominant game, forcing Jasper to hurt him. The stench of the other's defeat had remained on him, only angering Jasper that much more. The scent of the morning's freshly baked goods pulled him through the quaint and welcoming door, and the slender goddess who served him brought thoughts of a different form of servicing to mind.

Slightly above average in height – he would guess about five foot seven – she was the perfect height to settle against his body. For someone who owned and operated a bakery, she was as skinny as a rail. However, if he looked close enough he could see the telltale signs possible of curves. And with just a little bit of his help and pampering she would gain some well-needed cushion. No matter what, she'd look amazing underneath him. Her long, light brown hair curled in a bun on the top of her head. His fingers ached to pull out the pins and watch it tumble down her back. Hazel eyes sought him and begged for his protection. Damn, he was willing.

Her look made the wolf within him perk up and growl.

"Mate? I want her". His wolf paced beneath the surface of his skin, calculating the best way to quickly claim their mate.

What his wolf spoke of was a possibility. There were only a few women in the world through time that carried the scent to signal the potential mating. Unlike his brother Kade, who had met two women recently that carried the scent, Jasper had never in his one-hundred and three years come across a woman who brought forth the mating urge. However, if all encounters were like this one, Jasper didn't know how others walked away. The urge rode him hard and he fought his wolf for control if only for a moment, something that hadn't happened since he was a pup.

He mentally spoke to his wolf. *"We are not ready for a*

mate. And a human no less. She knows nothing of us. If, and that is a big if, we chose her to be our mate, we will have to go slowly into this. I don't want us to scare her. But she is beautiful, no"

His wolf growled in response.

"Do you want to scare her away? Let's get to know her first, see if she is a good match, other than that incredible cinnamon scent. I'll talk to Adam and find out everything I can about her. I am the Beta; I cannot put my Pack in jeopardy."

God, he really sucked at this. This time he needed to put on his big wolf panties and actually ask her out.

"Then we could mark her."

He snorted at his wolf. Yeah, that was taking it slow.

Jasper shook himself from his inner thoughts and looked into those hazel eyes. The spot of flour on her cheek begged for his hand to brush it way. He fought the urge. No need to freak her out. Her chest moved slowly, her small breasts rising and falling. The cinnamon scent of her filled his nostrils and he took a deep breath, the aroma going straight to his cock. The slight gasp that escaped from her kissable lips almost broke his control, and he fisted his hands to regain it.

"Good morning." His voice lowered an octave and became a growl. He cleared his throat and started again. "I come here every morning and I don't think I ever gave you my name. Let me rectify that." He closed the distance between them so only the counter separated them. "I'm

Jasper Jamenson. It's a pleasure to meet you." He held out his hand in hopes of touching her skin.

Willow blinked up at him and seemed at a loss for words. Her lips opened slightly, begging him to lean down and taste her.

"Uh... yeah... I'm Willow Delton." She shook her head, gave him a small smile and placed her slender hand in his. He'd been right – her skin was incredibly soft and made him want to take a bite.

"Yes, I know, you own this place." He gave her hand a squeeze and released her.

"So, Jasper, do you want your usual?" The sound of his name on her lips hardened his cock. Without waiting for him to respond, she turned back to her work-table to ice her cinnamon rolls.

"Sounds good." He watched as her hands moved swiftly and confidently across the baking sheets. "What time do you get off?"

"Smooth, Romeo. Why don't you just ask her to bend over the work table for you?"

Ignoring his wolf Jasper continued, "I thought that we could grab a bite to eat tonight and go see the arts fest they have running in town."

Oh dear Lord. Why didn't he ease into this?

"Oh, are you asking me out on a date?" She wrinkled her brow and looked utterly confused at the prospect.

"Yes, I am. I've been in here for over a month every

morning, and as much as I love your food, I had an ulterior motive."

Surprise flashed across her face before her eyes lit up with excitement. "I've never been to the arts fest in town. I didn't want to go by myself and didn't have anyone to go with me." Her mouth snapped shut at her revealing statement.

Laughing quietly, he shook his head. "So what time do you get off?"

"You really need to stop putting it like that; it gives me ideas." Again, he ignored his wolf's sarcasm.

"I close at four and should be done cleaning up by five. It's only me here today so it's going to take me an hour to close."

"What do you say I come back at six and we go to dinner from here?"

Her smile almost blinded him as she nodded before taking off her apron. "Okay. Sounds good. Here's your breakfast." She handed him his black coffee and a small brown bag with a pink logo.

Taking everything from her hands, he set them down along with the cash to pay for it. Giving into temptation, he leaned over the counter to brush the flour from her cheek.

She jumped and a flash of alarm raced across her face.

Chuckling under his breath, he reassured her. "Just some flour. I'll see you at six, Willow." He grabbed his breakfast and walked to the door, taking one last look behind him at the woman who was his mate. He was one lucky bastard.

Whistling a jaunty tune, he walked toward his Jeep, unconcerned and happy while leaving his mate to do her work. The hairs on the back of his neck lifted, and his wolf came to attention. The street was empty but for a few people; nothing looked out of place. Jasper took a deep breath but didn't detect another presence. With one last look toward his slender brunette, he shrugged off the uneasy feeling and continued to his Jeep.

2
———

The man of Willow's dreams walked out the door but this time was coming back for her. She had a date with Jasper. Her heart pound in her ears, and she felt like jumping up and down like a teenager. She bit her lip, holding back a squeal. Probably not the best time to do that.

Jasper – the name suited him. Unique, yet strong. Closing her eyes to savor the feel of his presence, she tried to recall every word he'd said, every move he' made. The warmth from his fingertips still tingled against her cheek. She took a deep breath of his lingering male scent and steadied herself before opening her eyes. An older couple stood staring at her with their lips pursed and brows furrowed. She must have been completely out of it not to hear the bell.

"I'm so sorry. I'm just having one of those days. What

can I get for you? I have fresh cinnamon rolls for you if you like." She couldn't wipe the grin off her face and helped them to begin her day.

Breakfast and lunch flew by. Cleaning the few tables inside her shop, she hummed to herself as she thought about the night to come. She had a date. The small mountain town they lived in had a decent selection of potential matches. But from what she's observed, they were players or married. Sometimes both. Not until Jasper walked into her bakery, had she noticed a man. And oh, did she notice.

Suddenly the hair on her arms stood on end and she tensed. Someone was in the bakery. Why the hell hadn't she heard that damn bell? She turned quickly and bit off a gasp. A large man stood almost directly behind her, blocking her path. He glared down at her with a malicious curl to his lips. Tension and danger ebbed from him.

Letting this man know he scared her would be a mistake.

"Can I help you? I'm about to close, but I still have a few baked goods that are fresh and good to go." *Subtle, Willow. Let's try not to let the scary man know he is terrifying, shall we?* At least her voice didn't shake.

The stranger hadn't moved or spoken a word. He was at least as tall as Jasper and had the same hair color, but the similarities stopped there. Where Jasper was handsome in his masculine looks, this man was anything but. His hard face sported a nose that might have been broken, but never set. His lips gave an almost perpetual snarl. He was beefy, muscular, and downright scary. With his presence, any happiness and confidence Willow had gained that day evaporated.

"Let me just go behind the counter—" *Where access to the back door is.* "—and I can help you with whatever you need." Her voice started to crack, and she walked quickly, trying to get away from him.

Just as she reached the counter, his hand shot out and grasped her upper arm in a painful grip.

"What are you – ?"

He shook her hard, her body whipping around like a rag doll, and ended her sentence before he pulled her toward him.

"You smell just like him. He shouldn't have done that. If he really cared for you he wouldn't have marked his scent then left you all alone." His breath was rancid and crawled against her ear as he growled at her.

What is he talking about?

"Please let me go. I don't know what you're talking about."

She punched him in the gut. Years of living in foster homes taught her quite a bit. He grabbed her hip and rubbed himself on her while licking her ear. Gagging, she twisted and tried to scratch him. He only pulled her closer and rocked his erection against her.

As she opened her mouth to scream, he let go of her arm and closed his hand over her mouth.

"Nuh uh, little girl. No screaming or I will make you suffer longer before I kill you. You are a pretty thing, though a little skinny for my taste. Not enough tit to grab onto, but you'll do. That fucker thinks he can claim you for his mate? Fuck him. You are going to be mine, at least for a little while before we tear you to pieces." He smiled and lifted his hand from her mouth to give her a bruising kiss.

She resisted, but he held her head to him by pulling her hair and rocked again. His erection brushed her, and she shuddered. Tears streamed down her face as she whimpered in pain.

Just then, the back door slammed open and another stranger came barreling in. The man wasn't as tall as her assailant, but he looked similar, except for the jagged scar running along his face.

"Shit, Isaac, stop fucking around. If the Redwoods know we're on their territory they'll tear our throats out. Not to mention it reeks of the Beta in here. Once he finds out, there'll be hell to pay. Just get the bitch in the car and don't fuck with her. She's the Alpha's first. Once Hector gets a taste, you can have her. Assuming there is anything left."

"Fuck you, Reggie. I can do whatever I damn well please with this tasty piece."

The man named Reggie glowered at Isaac. "Get the fuck

in the car, dude. I'll gut you if I have to." Isaac buckled under an unknown force and Willow gasped.

Oh my God. What's going on? What is that?

Was it a Taser? No. She didn't see one.

Oh God. What was happening?

As he shifted again, Willow tried to break free.

"No, pet, I don't think so." His dry tongue licked the side of her face. Bile rose in her throat.

Oh God, she didn't want to die.

"You're coming with us. And when that fucking Beta Jasper gets wind we have you, then we can kill him too." Reggie strolled across the room toward the two of them.

The fist came at her face too fast to register until she felt a painful explosion against her cheek.

The last thing she remembered was wondering where they were taking her and what did Jasper, her dream man, have to do with it?

3
———

"You look so cute dressed up. Willow isn't going to know what hit her." Melanie, Kade's mate, bounced around Jasper's living room helping him to choose his clothes for his date with Willow.

A growl sounded behind him, and Jasper laughed out loud.

Yep, his older brother was a tad bit possessive.

"Hey, man, it's the truth." Jasper ducked when a pillow from his couch flew by his head.

"Oh stop being a baby, Kade." Mel's eyes danced. "He's handsome, and he's going on his first date with his mate. There's no reason to be jealous. In fact, the better he looks, the more likely he is to come home with his mate. Once he's all marked and mated, it'll be one less male you have to growl at." Mel sauntered up to Kade and whispered in his ear. Whatever she said must have been good because Kade's eyes darkened as he took his wife's mouth. A smidge of jealousy settled in Jasper's stomach. Hopefully, he was about to do the same with Willow.

After a few minutes of them going at it, Jasper threw a pillow at them. "Seriously, you two need to get a room, and not one in my house." He grinned and tucked his black button-down shirt into his new dark jeans. Jasper also had on his favorite black boots and kept his hair down. Whenever he refrained from his typical ponytail and left his shoulder-length hair loose and half-dried after a shower, the scent of Willow's interest increased. He wanted to keep that up.

"Fine, fine. But I don't want to hear anything when I do the same to you and Willow once she gets here." Kade slapped his back in brotherly love, and Mel gave him a comforting hug before leaving him alone with his nervous thoughts.

He shouldn't be nervous. Willow was his mate. Fate had designed them for each other. Though there were others that had the potential to be his mate, Willow was it for him. Her cinnamon scent had seeped into his soul. She was his.

We will take care of her every need and pleasure her beyond comprehension. No problem.

Jasper snorted at his wolf. "You really need to stop saying shit like that. She's human. This is going to be hard enough seeing how I have never mated before, and I don't want to fuck this up. But add on the fact that I'm opening her eyes to a world of supernaturals from her nightmares... Yeah, this could go poorly." That was the last thing either of them needed.

His younger brother, Adam, strode through the door without knocking, as all of his family was known to do. Over a hundred years of being together had dissolved most boundaries. "Jasper man, you really need to stop talking to yourself. And don't worry. Just be yourself and everything will work out. On second thought, just be me."

"I was just talking to my wolf. I don't like talking in my head all the time. I look like a nutter, rather than just sounding like one." As a werewolf, he shared a body with a wolf spirit much older than he. And if he asked this wolf, much wiser, too. The man was more dominant and chose when to shift, but the wolf always had an opinion. When he was in wolf form, he sometimes let his wolf take charge on a hunt, but Jasper was always present.

Jasper took a drink of water from the pitcher in the fridge and flipped Adam off. "And fuck you. You keep your dumbass away from my mate."

And if he touched her, then Adam would pay. Maybe he'd make him watch *From Justin to Kelly* then put Icy Hot on his balls.

Adam laughed and took a glass of water for himself. Adam was only about an inch shorter than him, and other than Adam's shorter hair, they could pass for twins.

"You don't need to worry about that. I know when some-one's staked his claim. But I do need a favor from you." Adam straightened when he spoke as an Enforcer, rather than his brother.

"What's up?" Jasper fell into his role of Beta, though thoughts of Willow were not far from his mind.

"One of the adolescents took a stroll through the woods near Main Street, where Willow's bakery is, and thought he smelled something. It could be nothing, but I need to check it out. I figured since you were going down there anyway, I'd catch a ride with you and then wolf it back to search for scents."

Jasper's body went on alert. His heart beat in his ears. "When did you hear this? Why the fuck did you wait until now to come and get me? My scent is all over that bakery. If some lone wolf goes near Willow, they're just going to think she's meat. I haven't claimed her yet." Jasper could feel his wolf prowl, ready to attack the dangers surrounding his mate.

"Calm down. I just heard about it before I walked here. We can go together to check out the threat. But as I said, the pup wasn't sure what he smelled. He wasn't sure if it was a wolf or not. But seeing how it's close to Willow's, I thought we should go."

Jasper grabbed his keys and had left the house before Adam had time to take another breath. He needed to check on her. If anyone came near her or even sniffed her, he'd kick some ass.

"Let me drive, man," Adam said as he reached the driveway. "I don't want you to take us off the road. You're a little edgy now."

Jasper tossed him the keys and climbed into the passenger seat of his Jeep.

THE SMELL of other wolves reached his nose before his eyes registered the front door ripped off its hinges. He jumped from the Jeep before it stopped, with Adam following close behind. Jasper entered the bakery and took in the scene. Broken chairs lay on their sides among wooden splinters and gouges on the floor. Glass shards littered the carpet, creating a landscape of destruction.

"Mate?"

His wolf clawed to the surface, begging to be let out. The need to find her and demand retribution rode Jasper hard. Fuck. He'd kill anyone who dared lay a hand on her.

Jasper took a deep breath. There wasn't any blood. Thank God she wasn't bleeding. She could still be injured, but it was a good sign there wasn't blood. Two wolves had been there. Their scent lingered. But they weren't lone wolves. No, worse. They were from his Pack's rivals – the Central Pack.

His soul fractured as his heart clenched. His blood

boiled and his temples throbbed. He slammed his fist into the wall and growled in agony. He was too late.

"Where is she, Adam? Why the fuck did they take her? How the hell did the Centrals get in our territory and take my mate?" He breathed heavily and paced throughout the chaos.

"I don't know, Jasper, but believe me, we're going to find her then kill any wolf that touched her." Adam had lost a mate years before when a rival attacked her. Jasper knew he would do anything to save Willow.

Adam was already on the phone with their father and brothers while Jasper searched for any clue. The Centrals were ruthless, and their leader, Hector Reyes, was a sadistic bastard who believed in the superiority of wolves over humans and witches. There were rumors he'd killed his wife when she tried to protect their daughter from being sold.

Adam closed his phone and caught Jasper's attention." North and Reed on are their way. Mom and Dad are going to stay behind with Cailin, Mel, Kade, and Maddox, as well as the stronger of the Pack's wolves to protect the territory in case this is just the first assault. The four of us will go to Central territory to retrieve her."

Jasper should have thought more for Willow's safety. He should have put plans to protect her in place. He hadn't even marked her. He'd already failed his mate. Once he saved her, and he would, he'd make sure he never failed her again. No matter what.

"They're going to be here soon," Adam said. "We need to get outside. Are you ready? We're about to violate the treaty by entering their territory without permission."

Like he gave a shit. He paced the length of the room, his muscles twitching with anxiety and aggression. Barely suppressing the urge to pound another fist into the nearest wall, he said, "They came here and kidnapped her. I have no idea if she's alive or dead. We aren't fully mated; she doesn't carry my mark. I can't feel her in here!" He slapped his fist to his chest above his heart.

A stormy look flashed across Adam's face, and Jasper immediately regretted his tirade.

"I'm sorry, Adam, I wasn't thinking about Anna. I'm so sorry."

"It's okay, Jasper. I, above all, know what you are feeling now. But this will be different. We're stronger now. We will find her." Adam gave him a rough hug before he left the shop. The sound of a car outside signaled the arrival of his brothers. Time to kick ass and find his mate.

4

———

slam of a car door woke Willow.

Where am I? What happened?

Head pounding, her thoughts collided then slowly coalesced. The scratchy surface of a torn fabric rubbed against Willow's bound wrists behind her back. She craned her neck to the side and discovered faded upholstery. She was in the backseat of a car. *Well, at least I'm not in the trunk.* Sarcasm aside, terror churned in her belly. An unwelcome friend in a dire situation.

Why couldn't she be the kick ass heroine of one of those newer, cheesy romance novels? She could take the knife tucked in her boot, free herself, and kill anyone in her path. Okay, maybe not kill, but seriously maim nonetheless.

Willow inwardly winced. Damn, she was officially going crazy. Who were those men that had taken her? Isaac and

Reggie. That's right. What did they want with her? She was just a bakery owner with no family to speak of.

Jasper.

They'd tossed his name about before they knocked her out. But why? What did he have to do with it?

The car door opened abruptly, the sound of the metal grinding against metal piercing Willow's ears. Her breath stopped, fear taking over.

"She's awake." A man – no Isaac – spoke to people she couldn't see before leaning in the car. He reached beneath her to pull Willow out by her tied hands. The rope dug into her flesh, and she felt the faint trickle of warm liquid down her hands. Oh God, they'd broken the skin. A whimper escaped her, as Isaac pulled her to his chest.

"You smell sweet. We're going to have fun with you." Like in her shop, his breath assaulted her face. Distress trailed up her chest, seeping into her bones. *Don't let this man be the last face I see, please.*

He pulled her, not at all struggling with her weight, toward a drab gray building.

A wolf walked out the door, leading her down a dimly lit hall.

They keep wild animals here?

The wolf growled, then its body rippled. Its bones crunches and muscles tore, finally reshaping into a naked man.

"Hello, Willow. I'm Hector, the Alpha, leader of the

Centrals. And I'm going to be the last thing you see." He smiled.

Willow screamed as he backhanded her, throwing her into the wall. At the sound of the man called Hector's laughter, she fell into blessed darkness with some last conscious thoughts.

Werewolves are real.

And they are going to kill me.

BRACING HERSELF, Willow cracked open only her right eye because her left one had been swollen shut and took in her surroundings. Water trickled down the aging stone walls and dripped against concrete floors. A draft from the small crack under the door cooled the room and froze Willow's bones. She was locked in a basement or cellar of some sort with no windows and only a steel door as a way out.

The handcuffs currently digging into her wrists and ankles deterred any thought of moving. Hector had knocked her out cold with his fist, and she hadn't woken until they dropped her on the cold floor, naked and chained with a collar around her throat. The lack of an ache between her thighs was a blessing as she knew she'd escaped being raped – for now.

After trying to stay awake for what seemed like hours, she drifted in and out of consciousness until hands tugged at her chains, jostling her awake again.

"Get up," a gravelly voice ordered. "Time to speak to the Alpha."

What was an Alpha? Why couldn't she sleep? Her eyes felt heavy and exhaustion pulled at her, but she couldn't rest. Oh God, she didn't want to see the werewolves again.

Trying to conserve the last of her dwindling energy, she let them drag to a room on one of the upper floors.

"Ah, my pet. I'm happy to see you here. I'm Corbin, the Alpha's son." He smiled a cruel smile and Willow curled up into a ball. His hands rubbed along her arms and legs, trailing her stomach and breasts.

She fought the urge to shudder.

Oh God. This isn't happening.

"Little human, do you know why we took you?" Another voice spoke and Corbin lifted his hands.

Willow lifted her head, following the sound of the voice to meet the eyes of their Alpha.

Little human? Oh God. It wasn't a nightmare.

Although something inside told her to lower her eyes in submission, she refused to give him the satisfaction. Most likely of Hispanic ancestry, he looked to be about thirty-five with tan skin and mangy brown hair. His eyes were such a deep black they sent shivers down her body. Dressed in slacks and an expensive button down shirt, he didn't look like the gang leader she'd thought him to be. He looked more like a muscular business man on his way to a lunch meeting.

The slap across her face echoed through the room and forced her to whimper.

"Lower your eyes, bitch! You are not fit to be in my presence, let alone to look into my eyes. You're lucky I don't kill you on the spot. But then that would be putting an end to my fun, wouldn't it? No, little human, you're going to be my toy to play with before we kill you. Then your Jasper is going to know who is master won't he?" No longer did he sound the angry leader, he sounded like a malicious, sadistic man. Bile rose in her throat as her fear almost overpowered her. He gave her a menacing snarl then tugged at the chain on her collar to pull her toward him.

"Would you like to see what is going to kill you?"

He nodded toward to the man who'd abducted her, Isaac, who began to strip. Long scars trailed down his body and Willow tried to turn away. Hector tugged at her chain again and forced her to watch. Isaac bent at the waist and knelt. Willow gasped as the sounds of bones breaking and shaping resounded throughout the room and hair sprouted through his skin down his arms and torso. The bones on his face angled and lengthened to resemble a snout. His body heaved and twisted as he completed the change. Where Isaac had stood as a man, now an enormous golden eyed, black wolf hunched. The wolf threw back his head and howled, sending shivers down her spine and goose bumps along her arms.

Willow screamed.

Screamed and screamed while trying to scramble way. The leader only pulled on the chain harder.

"You will die by his claws and teeth. You will be begging for death before he is through with you, little woman."

He tugged on the collar again, cutting off her breath. *Dear God, please save me.* As she fell to floor with black spots dancing across her vision, the wolf crawled on top of her. Drool dripped down her body. She reached out, trying to reach for an escape that wasn't to be found and blessedly passed out.

WILLOW SHOT UP and winced as pain lanced through her body. Memories of what had transpired flooded her mind. She was locked in a den of werewolves. The monsters of her nightmares were real and on other side of the door ready to kill her after they – she gulped – played. Willow had always thought she was stronger than most, but even this was too much for her.

Tears wet her cheeks as she begged God for a chance. Please God, let Jasper find her and save her. She was alone in a cold, dark room with no chance of escape. Sorrow enveloped her. *Please, Jasper. Come.*

Jasper.

The Alpha had taken her because he had a feud with her mystery man. What had he done to deserve that wrath? What did she even know of him? What little she'd overheard during her stay led her to believe that he, too, was a werewolf. But he'd been near her for weeks and never hurt her. Why would that cruel man take her to hurt him?

When Jasper came, he'd be answering her questions.

If he came for her.

Willow took a deep breath and flinched at the pain in her ribs. Damn. They were probably broken. She needed a doctor.

Finally closing her eyes, she calmed herself and curled into a ball. Suddenly the door broke away from its hinges and flew across the room. She gasped in terror.

"Willow." Her name was a growl but relief flooded through her.

Jasper.

He came.

"Willow. Oh baby. Let me get you unchained." Jasper knelt down and brushed his hand against the bruises on her face. Unwillingly, she flinched, and he froze. Cursing under his breath, he growled again before reaching for her chains.

The sound of metal crunching and grating hurt her ears, but Jasper removed the cuffs from her wrists and ankles. Her skin prickled, and pain shot up her arm as the blood flowed freely again. She moaned and bit her lip.

"I know it hurts Wil, but let me get this collar off you and then I'll take you home. I'm so sorry baby, I..." He choked off the last words as tears fell from his eyes.

He was crying for her? He couldn't be all that bad for a werewolf.

"I'm going to put my shirt around you and then pick you up. It's going to hurt, Wil, so brace yourself." His eyes, still glassy from unshed tears, gazed into hers.

Jasper laid his shirt over her, tucking it around her. Pain shot through her body as he gently, oh so gently, cradled her nearly clad body to his chest. His lips caressed her forehead, and he took a ragged breath.

"Let's go home, baby. Reed, go start the car and, North, I want you in the back with us to check her when we head out. Adam, make sure you stay behind us and watch our backs."

Willow finally noticed the three men that joined them in her cell. Even in the dark, she could tell they were Jasper's brothers. The same green eyes filled with looks of pure anger stared back at her. The one called Reed was much skinnier with sandy blond hair. He nodded once and lowered his gaze before jogging out of the room.

From the corner of her eye she recognized Adam. He'd come into her shop with Jasper a couple of mornings, but he'd kept his distance, much like he was doing now. Willow strained her neck to see the last brother, North, who also looked like Jasper but with less muscles and dark blond hair. He seemed to be checking her body for injuries from across the room, and with each surveying glance, the anger in his eyes intensified. Though deep down she knew the anger wasn't directed at her, she still shuddered and buried her face into Jasper's chest. He smelled of forest and man, yet underneath, there was another scent – wolf.

Jasper held her closer and rubbed his cheek across the top of her head. She could feel the beat of his heart against her cheek, and as his breathing slowed, so did hers. Jasper would protect her. She had to believe that.

"I'm taking you home, Wil." When he took a step toward the door, she winced, and he froze.

"Did I hurt you? What can I do?"

She shook her head and shivered. It hurt all over, but being in his arms was worth it. He hadn't told her how he'd got here, and she didn't want to face what was out there.

Jasper's grip tightened for only a fraction of a second before it loosened. "They aren't out there, Wil. They were gone when we got here. I think they knew we were coming and left you here for dead." They both winced at the truth of the statement. "We can talk more once I get you home, baby. Okay?" She nodded against his chest as he followed North to Jasper's Jeep, Adam close behind.

Willow had almost fallen asleep in Jasper's arms when they stopped suddenly. Jasper's growl vibrated against her cheek. She looked up, and her heart stopped. They were surrounded by wolves and men – at least thirty bodies. Panic crawled up from her toes as she opened her mouth to scream. Only Jasper's voice prevented her.

"Don't make a sound. They can hear even your heart-beat. I will protect you. We all will."

A cackle of the most grotesque sort swept through the surrounding forest.

"I wouldn't be so sure, Beta. You will not live past the hour." The deep voice surrounded them, but Willow couldn't see who it came from.

Jasper growled again and North moved to cover them. She could hear Adam's heavy breathing behind them through her haze of pain and knew he must have moved closer as well. The pounding in her head and the men around them took all her concentration.

The Alpha stepped forward to glare at the three of them.

"I have a proposition for you." Hector, took another step toward them, smiling. "As much as I want to kill you and drink the marrow from your bones, this human scrap has entertained me. She is untainted and unclaimed. You give her to me and I will let your wolves go. For now. I have plans for this little human." His smile was cruel, and Willow almost vomited with fear.

Would Jasper give her to them? In doing so, he'd save himself and his brothers. He hardly knew her and had only asked her out. They hadn't even kissed or been on a date. She was nothing to him, and his brothers' lives were on the line. She knew the choice he would have to make and she didn't want to make it any harder for him or herself.

She tried to wiggle down from his arms to let them live.

Jasper's hold tightened a moment before letting her go. Blood rushed from her head and her heart shattered.

He let her go.

She was to be the sacrifice. Holding in a whimper from the pain of standing and a broken heart, she tried to keep herself steady. Jasper held onto her shoulder and when she tried to take a step away from him, he brought her closer to his chest.

She needed to get away from him. Death hunted for her, but she couldn't look at him, for he would see the betrayal she felt.

Stop being ridiculous.

Choosing his family was the right choice. Betrayal shouldn't be a consideration.

"I see." Jasper's voice lowered to a rougher edge. Willow dared a glance over her shoulder and gasped at his face. She'd been right, he was a werewolf. His upper canines had elongated, and a ring of gold had formed around the forest green of his eyes. But she wasn't afraid of him. Not this wolf.

Jasper growled under his breath, and she flinched. "Then I guess I must claim her now."

Before she could register the shock of his comment, Jasper tugged her to his chest and bit down on the curve of her shoulder where it met her neck. When his teeth punctured her flesh, she felt and heard a distinctive pop, before pain shot through her system. The bite deepened, and he held on, growling all the while. Willow's knees gave out, and she would have collapsed to the ground if not for Jasper's hands holding her up. He rocked against her and she felt his rock hard erection against her ass.

He's tearing into my flesh and getting off on this?

Panic flooded her.

But then a curious tingling swept over her. Peace and sex. Like honey, the feeling flowed through her blood and body to her head and breasts, then down to her stomach and womb before tickling her toes. Gasping, she held on to Jasper for stability as she came against him in front of thirty angry wolves and his brothers.

Her juices flowed down her legs as the men surrounding her flared their nostrils in excitement. Some broke formation to rub the evidence of their arousal, awakening her from her sexual fog.

Jasper released her shoulder, licked the wound, then nuzzled her cheek. Heat climbed her face as she became of aware of what had just happened. Jasper had bit her, and she'd orgasmed. *What the hell?*

A roar of pure rage and hatred echoed through the mountains.

"Fucking Beta! You think that just because you're a Jamenson you can defy me? You fucking claimed her? I'll kill you. But first I'll take that bitch, rape her and beat her in front of you!" Hector screamed, spitting out his words in pure fury. He opened his mouth to condemn them again, but was suddenly flying through the air after being smacked by the front of Jasper's Jeep. The crunch of gravel beneath the tires was the only warning they'd had.

The Jeep skidded to a halt in front of them. Adam threw himself into the front while North grabbed Willow by the arms, ignoring her wounds, and jumped into the back. Jasper followed close behind. He'd barely landed in the seat before Reed drove off into the forest like a maniac.

"Fuck!" Reed roared as he drove on. "He had you mark her? In front of them? Fuck, man! Fuck!" Reed's knuckles whitened against the wheel as he drove. He looked in the mirror and cocked his head. "The wolves aren't following us. I don't know what's going on, but it's like they're stuck there. Is some unseen force holding the other wolves back? Why would they do that? That wasn't wolf or witch magic, man, but I don't fucking know what it was. That was something deep. We gotta tell Dad."

What were they talking about? First werewolves and now magic. Her head spun.

Jasper pulled her off North and laid her across his lap. His warmth swept through her, seeping into her bones. She curled into his body, his arms cradling her.

Reed panted and talked fast as the adrenaline sped through his system. Willow reached over the seat and touched his arm. Startled, he swerved off the road, before righting himself and looking toward her.

"Thank you for coming back." Her voice was raw, and it hurt to move, but it needed to be said.

"Yeah, man, thanks." North nodded toward Reed and began to examine her, though it was difficult as she still lay across Jasper's lap. His pokes and prods made her wince and moan. With every flinch, Jasper's growls grew louder, and his arms tightened.

"And thank you North and Adam. It's nice to see you. Well, not nice, but..." She was rambling and she knew it. She looked up at her savior and tried to hide her heart. He couldn't know how deeply she felt for him. "Thank you, Jasper." She choked off a sob, and his hold tightened almost painfully.

"I need to breathe." She tried to smile, but she knew it came out like a grimace.

His hold loosened immediately, and he rubbed his hand against her ass. "Sorry." His voice roughened. The anger in his eyes hurt her already wrecked heart. That bite had meant something, and they'd forced him into it. She didn't know what the future held, but Jasper had been coerced into doing something he didn't want and he would only resent her for it.

"I think she has some broken ribs, Jasper," North said. "But other than the bruising and a few cuts, I don't think there's anything else broken. I won't know until we get back to the den and my equipment." North stopped touching her and immediately Jasper's shoulders relaxed.

They rode for over an hour before Jasper finally broke the silence.

"We're almost at the den, Reed and Adam, you both need to tell the Pack what happened. North, Willow and I will join you at your clinic, and you will check her for deeper injuries." His brothers nodded in agreement. Willow was surprised they didn't question Jasper's demands.

I wonder what that means.

Willow burrowed into Jasper's side. He may have been angry with her, but cold had leached into her bones, and only Jasper's intense body heat could warm her.

With one decision, the world opened up and tried to swallow her whole. She'd said yes to Jasper's invitation and the bad men came. The things that went bump in the night had captured her and almost killed her. Their rescue had provided safety for her through their power. For now she was going to the wolf's den, where the monsters lived. Her heart may be broken and the man she barely knew and had fallen for might resent her, but he was her savior. She'd cling to that and his warmth for as long as she could.

5

Jasper looked out the Jeep's window, his gaze on the passing trees. The Redwood Pack's den lay in a valley where two mountains converged deep within the forest. It was Jasper's home, his oasis. Protected on three sides by nature, the Den reflected a symbol of strength and longevity. Something he desperately fought to preserve in his role as Beta. When the battle between demons and werewolves had ended over a thousand years before, the first of Jasper's ancestors settled in the forest, mistakenly thinking the ancient large trees redwoods. The misinterpretation had given them their moniker and had long since been a token of humor within the Pack.

Jasper took a deep breath, watching the scenery in a blur. Trees and greenery filled the den. Wildflowers burst with color among the bushes and gardens surrounding some homes and landmarks. Homes were spread about and hidden below the canopy to allow individual privacy. In the center of town, brick buildings and small shops rose up from the expansive gardens. In the northern plain, large rock formations created the circle where meetings and dominance battles commenced. The first spiritual and magical settling of the Pack struck ground here. The pull of his family and Pack tugged on Jasper's heart – he was home. And his mate was by his side. Happiness swept through him.

Willow fell asleep before they arrived at the gates. The magical barrier that hid the den from outsiders slid over them as they passed through, their Pack connection acting like a key in a lock. It humbled him that she felt safe enough to fall asleep in his arms. But she probably wouldn't be sleeping if she knew what was forced on them. On her. Crawling through the underbelly of their fucked up world was not the best way to be introduced to ones future. His prior glee subsided a bit.

Jasper didn't know what was worse, the shattered and broken look on her face when she thought he would let her die or the pain that encompassed her when he bit her shoulder. The sensation of binding his wolf to her through the bite had nearly made him come at the same time as Willow had. Only the danger surrounding them stopped him. They were only bound through the mark, and their mating was incomplete. They still needed to consummate the relationship by him spilling his seed in her womb before their souls joined eternally.

The circumstances had stripped her choice. Now she was forever bound to him. He'd wanted to subtly coax her into his life and into his bed. That was no longer an option. They'd have to make love soon or the mating urge would take over his body and make him uncontrollably violent and nearly rabid. As it was, it rode him hard, and only the bruises on her face and heart stopped him. Never would he touch her again without her acceptance. Painfully, Jasper would wait and try his best to help her heal her and understand his world before taking that next step. He just hoped it didn't take too long.

His wolf snorted in agreement.

The gravel crunched beneath the tires as Reed pulled up to North's clinic. The one-story ranch home was one of the newer buildings in the den, but still had a rustic feel. Jasper carried his mate, cradled in his arms, inside and laid her down on the soft examining table. North followed silently behind them and bent over his patient. Jasper's wolf growled and bristled at his brother's nearness to his mate.

His wolf prowled to the surface. *"We marked our mate and need to finish it. Your brother is too close to her. His scent must not mingle with hers. That is our right and privilege."*

North merely lifted a brow but continued his work. All werewolves talked to their wolves, whether spoken aloud or not. North bandaged the bite on her shoulder, though with the enzyme in Jasper's saliva it would soon heal and not leave a scar.

The image of the bite was not what marked her; rather the bite allowed his scent to completely permeate in her skin forever. Unlike before in the bakery when his scent merely touched her skin, now it was in her pores and in her cells. She would forever be his, and once she marked his shoulder, the same would be true of him.

Because she was human, his wolf only mated one-sided. When and if she transitioned and marked him, their wolves would be fully joined, as it was only his wolf was mated. As a man and woman, it would take the act of making love for their souls to bind. Werewolves were cohesive and volatile symbioses of two beings. It made sense that their mating would require two steps to complete.

"She has two broken ribs but no other internal injuries." North's voice pulled him from his thoughts. "I'm going to bind them now, but because of the mate mark, she should be healed within the next two days or so. The bruising and small cuts should be gone by then too. Other than being sore, I think she's going to be fine."

North removed his gloves and shook his head. "Physically anyway. I can only imagine how she is going to be mentally and emotionally. I know this isn't how you wanted to mate her, but like it or not, she is here, and she's yours. Do you know what you are going to do about it?" His voice held sympathy but none of the pity Jasper had been afraid would fall upon Willow.

Jasper took a breath and tried to release the anger building within. "She's mine. There's no question of that. I'll do whatever it takes for her to accept me and our world. Our Pack is important, and I'll protect it with my life, but now I have Willow and I need to protect her too." He let out a deep breath and walked toward her. Tracing the edge of her cheek with his finger, he felt the heat from healing, and he knew she would wake soon with questions.

"I'm going to take her home and get her cleaned. Hopefully by the time she wakes up, I'll have better answers for her." He gently picked her up and carried her to the door North held open for them.

"I don't envy you that conversation, bro. Dad most likely knows what happened. Be prepared for his visit, as well as Mom's. Dad's going to want to make sure you're all right and meet the mate you've chosen – not to mention the Central Pack needs to be taken care of. Mom will want to pamper Willow so they'll be in your hair." North's lips curled into a smirk, and he let them leave with a nod.

"Thanks, bro."

"Good luck."

WILLOW'S EYES FLUTTERED OPEN. Jasper knelt above her. His gaze roamed her body, though not in a salacious way. Probably checking her injuries. Her eyes met his, and she felt as if she'd come home. Pain radiated in her head as she shook the idea of him loving her from her mind. He'd been forced into protecting her, being with her.

They were in a bedroom that held a large wooden king-sized bed of a deep color and matching furniture. The walls and carpet were a warm honey that looked like they would wrap around her and soothe her to sleep.

The room was clean with only a few pictures of what she guessed were his family and a few hand-carved wooden animals and figurines. The room felt like it welcomed her home and again, she suppressed the feeling.

"Hey." Her voice sounded raspy and not at all like hers.

He blinked then brushed the tip of his finger against her brow. Her body shivered, and he pulled away.

"I don't know how to make this up to you, Wil. I have so much to tell you, but first, since you're awake, let's clean you up." Jasper stood and held out his hand. He helped her from the bed before leading her slowly to the bathroom.

He gently pulled off her shirt and paused. His chest rose and he growled, then shook his head. His hand fisted and he turned to start a warm bath. She stood there in his large and comfortable bathroom naked and vulnerable, but Jasper would never hurt her. For all of the new revelations and supernatural events she'd experienced in the past day, she trusted Jasper. Though it hadn't been the most romantic of circumstances, he'd held her naked in his arms not more than a few hours before. There was no need for modesty at this point.

"Let me help you." His hands were rough and calloused as he touched her hip and led her into the bath. The water steamed hot and stung her aching skin but after a moment, began relieving the soreness. She moaned as she knelt in the water, and the hand on her hip tightened.

"This feels good. Thank you, Jasper."

"That's nice to hear, Wil. I would put in some Epson salts to help, but I want to make sure we clean off this dirt and grime first." He held a washcloth in his hand and lathered it with soap. The scent of sandalwood tickled her nose. She grinned at the smell. Jasper's smell.

He cleaned her body with gentle care and no words. The cloth brushed over her nipples, and she looked up, but he didn't stop, nor did he stop when he delved between her legs slowly and leisurely, washing her in her most intimate place. Though he touched her in a way no other man had in a long time, he didn't make it sexual, merely cleaned the night away from her skin.

He turned on the hot water again and rinsed her body then washed her hair. Once clean, he lifted her from the bath and patted her dry with a soft, fluffy towel. Her muscles felt weak, heavy. He put one of his shirts over her head, lifted her to his chest, and carried her to the bed.

Jasper finally spoke again as he laid her down. "I know you have many questions, but you need to rest. When you wake up, I'll answer anything you ask. I know this is not what you wanted, but we'll work it out. Just to warn you, my parents will be here soon, and they'll want to talk to you, so gain any energy you can from sleep, my Willow." He kissed her cheek and was about to lift himself from her when she placed her hand on his cheek.

"I trust you, Jasper. Thank you for coming for me." Her voice sounded calm, but firm. She couldn't have him thinking it was his fault, he was the one who was stuck with her.

Blinking once, he nodded and kissed her palm. He seemed to struggle with something before lowering his mouth to hers. His lips were soft and wet as he deepened the kiss. She gasped and opened her mouth to him before biting softly on his bottom lip. He growled and pulled away.

Panting heavily, he shook and stood straight. "Rest well, Willow. I'll be here if you need me." He turned quickly and strode out of the room, taking her heart with him.

WILLOW WOKE up to the sound of voices in the hall. Before investigating, she slowly studied the room. She was still alone. She closed her eyes again, then reached her arms above her head and winced in pain.

Yep, still hurts.

Rolling her head around her shoulders, she stretched as best she could, trying to soothe some of her aches and pains. Someone had laid out sweats on the edge of the bed when she slept. She hauled herself up and put them on. Once in the bathroom, she got the first look of herself in the mirror and gasped.

Her eye was already black and blue, but oddly enough, the swelling seemed to have gone down. There were cuts and scrapes along her cheek and hairline, but the blood had been washed away by Jasper the night before. Lowering the neck of Jasper's shirt, she removed the bandage. She saw bruising around her throat in the shape of the collar placed around her neck and the impression of Jasper's bite that had saved her gave her shivers. The stark contrast between the heavy, dark purple bruising and the paleness of her skin scared her. The image in the mirror was not that of the baker and loner of the day before, but the survivor thrown into a new world. A world that scared her. But not Jasper. Only the thought of losing him did that.

The voices from outside the bedroom grew louder and she steadied herself to find them. She slowly walked to a large living area of dark brown and tan masculine furniture, the wood decorated with carvings. The room was mostly sparse except for Jasper and two others who looked to be his siblings.

Immediately they stopped talking. The topic of conversation must have been her. Jasper stood and took a step toward her. Before she could comprehend the worried look on his face, it cleared to a blank expression.

"Willow, did you sleep well?" Jasper stood before her and caressed her bruised cheek with his knuckles.

His touch left her mind in tangles, but she nodded. Her gaze wandered to the two quiet people who rose to their feet behind Jasper.

Jasper noticed the object of her gaze and smiled. "Wil, these are my parents, Edward and Patricia, most call her Pat though." He took her hand and linked their fingers before leading her to the young looking couple before her.

Jasper's mother was warmth and love personified. It practically radiated through her pores. She looked to be about five feet tall, and soft, motherly curves made her welcoming. Light brown hair with natural, almost blonde highlights and warm brown eyes only accentuated her beaming smile.

Jasper's father was a tall man, though not as tall as Jasper. With broad shoulders and similar build, he reminded her of his son. His hair was dark brown, lighter than Jasper's. His gaze rested on her, sizing her up and taking measure.

A soft growl broke the silence.

Jasper.

"Dad, Mom, this is my mate, Willow Delton." At the word mate, Willow stiffened. He'd called her that before, but she wasn't prepared for the casual ease at with which the word left his lips.

What exactly did that mean? Had he claimed her like an animal? Did he even want her?

"Hello, Willow Delton, it is good to meet the mate of my second son. I'm sure you have as many questions about us as we have of you. Please sit down." Edward's deep voice held no room for objection and waved her toward the couch.

"Dad, don't grill her."

"Oh, Jasper honey, we won't do that. We just want to get to know her, and I am sure, after last night, she has many questions. I mean she was just introduced to our world and none too nicely." Pat, smiled and took Willow's other hand in hers as Jasper sat beside her, close enough that their thighs touched and she felt the heat of him.

At Pat's comment, silence swept through the room. Willow didn't think she could take another strained and awkward silence, so she stepped up to the paranormal plate.

"So, I guess you guys are werewolves. I'm guessing shaving is a bitch." Her mouth shut with an audible snap as heat crept up her neck into her cheeks. What on earth had possessed her to say that? *Good job Willow. Tell the very big werewolves, who could snap you like the twig you're named after, that they have a hairy problem.*

Jasper's boom of laughter vibrated though the room,

and her tense shoulders relaxed. Pat too laughed, and the lines around Edwards's eyes crinkled in amusement.

"Yes, we're werewolves, but I have no problem shaving in the morning." Again, Edward almost cracked a smile, and Willow knew she'd taken a huge leap toward acceptance with this man.

Edward sobered before he continued. "There is much you need to know, and I'm sure Jasper can tell you some, but I'll begin. We are the Redwood Pack, and once Jasper completes the mating you, too, will be part of us." Willow's brow furrowed and she shot Jasper what she knew must be a confused look, but he only scowled at his father.

Wait. Completes the mating? Like sex? Oh, geez.

"We've been a Pack for over a millennium and I've been Alpha for over two hundred years." Her eyes widened at his age and the fact that he looked damn good for it. "There are many other positions in the Pack, and you'll learn them over time; however, I'm in charge. It is my first duty to express my deep sorrow and regret that you've been pulled into this world without your permission. However, since the choice was taken from you, we must move forward.

"Our lives are deeply entrenched in secrecy and now yours will be as well. All you know will have to be left soon, and you must come with us for your safety. We know you only have few connections to the human world, but even those must be severed." Willow was startled at the amount of information they possessed concerning her.

"I understand. At least I think I do. But what about my bakery?" It was the only thing she had to call her own and to show her accomplishments in life. Without it, she had nothing.

Edward shook his head. "For now I think it must remain closed, at least for your safety. In the future we can discuss your reopening, but we can't say as of yet. Your safety as Jasper's mate is more important to us."

Willow took a deep breath and resisted the urge to cry as pain radiated through her heart. She nodded but couldn't speak. Jasper squeezed her in comfort, and the tightness in her chest eased.

"I know, Willow, this is a lot to take in now, but it'll be okay. We will protect you. You also need to decide whether or not you want to change, as it is your choice and privilege as Jasper's mate." *Change? Like into a werewolf?* Again, Willow took a deep breath to process that bit of terrifying information.

The idea of werewolves still scared the crap out of her, she'd never seriously thought they could exist and now she was surrounded by them, having a real conversation. She wasn't even sure she'd wanted a man, but she had one – who was a bit more than a man. And they offered her a choice of becoming one...

Her mind spun and she rubbed her temples.

Edward leaned over the coffee table and patted her hand reassuringly. "There will be many people who want to meet with you, most of them family, and we will be having a Pack meeting soon to discuss what happened out in the woods. But, I welcome you to our family, Willow Delton."

Edward stood and nodded. Pat got up and gave her a warm and soft hug, careful of the bruises. "Welcome to the family my dear. We may have many sons, but I only have one daughter by birth and one by mating. I'm honored to call you my own, dear." She gave Willow a smile with watery eyes and left the house with her husband.

Still sitting, Willow thought about everything that had changed. Even with the preternatural energy that exuded from him, Jasper was a calming presence beside her and she knew, no matter how he might resent their bond, she would cherish and take care of him as long as she could.

6

———

The door clicked softly as it closed behind his parents and not for the first time since he'd met Willow, Jasper was at a loss for words and action.

"What can I do, Willow?"

"I've only seen wolves when they tried to kill me." She wrung her hands together and bit her lip.

Jasper winced.

"Can you change into one? I mean, can you show me your wolf?"

He exhaled. This was something he could do. "Are you sure I won't scare you anymore than you already are?"

She shook her head. "I don't think that could happen. But I need to see you. You're good and not evil and if I see you as a wolf, that might help. You know."

He nodded and stripped off his shirt.

Her eyes widened and he blushed like a school girl. "Oh, I need to get naked to be a wolf. I don't want to tear my clothes. Wolves don't really care about nudity. I mean, we don't walk around the den naked or anything, but when we change we don't get embarrassed. But I can go stand behind the couch or something."

She blinked then matched his blush. "No, you can stay where you are. I need to get used to it right?"

He grinned then stripped off his pants. He heard her gasp at his lack of underwear, but he didn't react. He couldn't. He only prayed his cock wouldn't stand at attention before he could change.

He stood straight, then looked directly in her eyes. She stared back, careful not to look below his chin and he smiled.

God, she is too cute.

Jasper pulled on his magic and let the change sweep over him. His bones broke then realigned, but he only felt a twinge of pain. He'd been changing into a wolf since he was three and was used to it. Fur sprouted along his skin and his face elongated into a muzzle.

Soon he stood as a black wolf on four paws, frozen under Willow's stare.

She stood, unblinking.

Shit. Was this too much? Did he lose her already?

Finally she blinked. "Jasper?"

He tried to nod, then sat. She took a step toward him

and held out her hand. He lifted his head so her palm rested on top. She backed up, then shook her head and sank her hand into his fur. He leaned into her touch, loving the way her soft hands wound through his fur.

"You're so soft."

Jasper leaned closer and relished her touch.

"You're such a beautiful wolf, Jasper."

Jasper leaned back then shifted back into a man. He knelt naked next to her body and she laughed.

"That's so cool."

He chuckled. "That's better than being scared, I guess."

"Definitely."

Jasper put his clothes back on and tried not to think about her small hands roaming his body. Again, he found himself at a loss for words.

Jasper's mind sprang into gear with the sound of her stomach growling. He jumped up. "How about breakfast?"

The rosy color that highlighted her cheeks at the sound of her stomach made her look damned cute.

"I'm starving. I haven't eaten since before I started work." She bit her lip as her eyes grew cloudy.

Damn. Life could change so quickly from one moment to the next.

"But let me cook. I mean I don't want to intrude on your home and take over. It's just that I love cooking, and I do it every morning to open the shop or on Sundays just for me." She gave him a small smile, and the wolf inside him, normally a ferocious male, melted. They both would do anything for her, and Jasper knew the decadent taste of her cooking well enough not to hold her back.

"If you are up to it, Wil. I love your food, but I don't want you to feel like you need to do anything for me. Ever. Especially if you are still feeling sore and achy." When she just grinned and nodded, he took her by the hand and led her to his kitchen.

Slightly over hundred years old, he'd lived in his house nearly as long. He'd updated it over the years to keep up with the times. He was still working on parts of it, and now that he had a mate, he knew they would need to expand with more space so she'd feel comfortable and there would be enough room for their pups.

The kitchen had been the first job he touched. He'd created a wide-open space with enough room for his large family to occupy. There were stainless steel appliances with dark wood cabinets and grey stone countertops. Masculine, even with the large island, but still homey to him and it melded with the forest outside.

Jasper led Willow to the large two-door refrigerator and opened it to reveal fairly stocked shelves. He didn't entertain or cook often, but when he did, he preferred a good, hearty meal.

"Is there anything you're interested in? I have everything you could possibly need for breakfast. At least I hope. I know you have more expertise in that area than I do."

Dear God. He was rambling like a teenager. Except for that one glorious kiss when he'd put her to bed, they'd barely touched. He knew many things about her, but she didn't know that much about him. That would have to change – and soon. She may have been forced into his world, but he would do his damndest to make her feel included and part of their Pack.

Willow studied his offerings like an artist would study a blank canvas before painting. In a matter of moments, he knew she'd cataloged his food and would come up with a perfect and delicious meal. Glancing up at him with a sly smile, she took out eggs, cheese, and veggies and set them on the island. With her second trip, she grabbed bacon, potatoes, and oranges.

He would have offered to help, and the man his mother raised begged him to, but he didn't want to interrupt her thought process. He loved the way she glided around the kitchen as if she'd been here all along. Even with the bruises, she was still gloriously beautiful and he knew through the mate mark she would heal any injuries quicker than a normal human. It was a one-time only perk of the bite and she wouldn't heal fast with other injuries until she changed.

If she changed.

"Do you think you can make orange juice and coffee?" Willow's soft request brought Jasper out of his thoughts. "I can do the rest, but I don't want to take over your kitchen completely."

"I can do that." He walked over to the cabinet and pulled out fresh gourmet coffee beans and put them in the grinder. Soon the smell of freshly ground coffee filled the air. He quickly set the automatic coffee maker to percolate and began slicing and squeezing oranges.

Willow moved around his kitchen with ease as she made breakfast. She broke the eggs against the side of the bowl before whisking them. He followed her hands as she moved quickly. The sound of fatty bacon popping and sizzling echoed in the kitchen, and she went back to the cutting board to slice onions and mushrooms for her omelets.

When he wasn't looking, she'd diced potatoes for home-made hash browns that were now browning on the stove-top. Already his mouth salivated at the thought of such a gourmet meal.

Like a magician, Willow prepared light and fluffy omelets bursting at the seams with bacon, spinach, mush-rooms, and feta and ricotta cheeses. On the each plate, she put three slices of bacon and still sizzling hash browns before he had time to put their drinks in mugs and glasses.

Thank God he was a werewolf because his arteries would be screaming if he was a normal human at his age.

Taking the plates from her hands, he set them on the table next to the drinks. Before she could protest, he took her face between his hands and placed a feathery light kiss to her lips. He lifted his head from hers, looked into her eyes, and gave her a smile.

"Thank you for breakfast. This has got to be the best meal I have ever seen made in this kitchen. I can't wait to see what you come up with here in the future."

At his startling reminder of their mating and future, her eyes widened and her lips parted. Jasper took this as another invitation to kiss her plump lips again. So he did.

When he pulled away, he smiled and said, "Let's eat."

Because if he didn't eat food, he'd want to indulge in her. And ravishing her against the kitchen table might not be the best way to slowly introduce her to this whole mating thing.

Willow bent over the table and set her plate down, her firm ass right near his crotch.

Jasper groaned. Yeah, this might be harder than he thought.

JASPER AND WILLOW walked the short distance to meet his family. Rather than worrying about all the questions still unanswered, she took in the scenery. Tall trees Jasper assured her were not redwoods surrounded them, and he told her the story of how his Pack had been was misnamed. Walking along the undergrowth over the worn paths, she felt as if she were in another world without city life. She snorted.

Yep, that pretty much covered it.

Though she'd been there less than a day, she'd already fallen head over feet in love with the den, and was well on her way to falling in love with the man beside her. If they gave her a chance, she'd feel right at home and never leave. A desire and need swept through her – the need to have a family, a home. She'd do anything she could to make this fairytale land hers.

Soon they reached another home with light beige paint and chocolate trim. Ivy crawled up the side, reminding her of an English cottage.

Willow took a deep breath to steady herself and she felt Jasper lightly squeeze her hand. She glanced up at him and froze.

His pupils were so large she could barely see the green rim. Though strength and honor shown through, she knew he'd do anything to protect her, even from his family. Something lurked in his gaze she couldn't quite grasp. That thought and reassurance staggered her.

Did he truly want her?

But before she could fully comprehend his look, the front door opened, and a beautiful blonde woman stepped out to greet them. Shorter than Willow, but curvier. She had a pert nose and large blue eyes, along with an ivory complexion and a welcoming smile.

Willow relaxed slightly.

"You must be Willow. I am so happy to meet you, even under these circumstances." Willow was immediately wrapped in a warm hug that wasn't too tight on her still sore ribs.

"Willow, this is Melanie, my sister-in-law," Jasper said.

"Let's get you in the house. You must need to sit down and rest." Melanie released Willow and took her hand to lead her inside. Willow gave Jasper an almost desperate glance over her shoulder, but he stared blankly before following them inside the home. Whatever look and feeling that passed between them before Melanie interrupted, was so far gone it was like it never happened. The achy feeling in her chest was no longer just from the pain of a few broken ribs.

Damn it. Why did Mel have to walk out of the house right at that moment? What was Jasper thinking? What did that look mean? Her arms tingled and her heart sped. God, she was in high school again, falling for the cute quarterback. But this time, did the object of her affection return her feelings?

Walking inside the house, she noted it was on the verge of melding two personalities. She could tell it had started out as a vastly masculine bachelor home. There were dark contrasts of deep greens and browns spread throughout the house, along with architectural drawings that looked to be hand-drawn.

From what she remembered from the rumors around town surrounding the sexy Jamenson family, Kade, Melanie's husband, was the part-owner of their family contracting and construction company. Kade served as architect, while Jasper was the second owner and main contractor. It was well known he liked to go in and work with his hands and get dirty when it came to wood-working. The hand carved figurines and other decorations around Jasper's home came to mind, and she almost gasped aloud at the immense talent he possessed.

Those hands could work wonders with wood. Wonder if they could work other places, too.

Shaking her head to return to the present, she took another step to fully enter the living room and immediately froze at the group of drool worthy model-like male flesh in the room.

The Jamenson brothers stood in front of her, and Willow didn't know what altar their parents had prayed to, but they'd all been blessed in good looks and build. Most gave her small smiles that she returned but one sat in the corner with a glare on his scarred face. A shudder went through her before Jasper placed his hand on the small of her back. Warmth spread through her, and she calmed.

Jasper's deep voice broke through the silence. "This is my mate, Willow. Willow, this is my family. You have already met Reed, Adam, and North." He nodded his toward each of them, and they returned the gesture while giving fuller smiles to her.

She raised her hand at a sad attempt at a wave before letting it fall. Talk about awkward. What could she say to the men who'd seen her naked and chained to a stone wall before saving her life then had witnessed the best orgasm of her life? Hallmark didn't make a card for that.

"You've just met Melanie, and this is her mate Kade, also my partner at the company," Jasper continued.

She looked up at the brother named Kade and saw a man who looked closer to Jasper in looks than the others. His hair was slightly lighter than Jasper's jet black, but darker than the rest of the brothers. They shared the same piercing green eyes and honey tan skin. He was also built and tall, but not as tall as Jasper. If anything she was sure Jasper was the biggest of the bunch. Good thing she liked big.

Kade came up to her with his hand extended and she placed her hand in his firm grip.

"I'm very happy that Jasper finally has someone to share his life with. I'm just sorry it had to occur this way. Melanie and I were lucky enough to meet relatively unscathed." He released her and put his arm around his mate's shoulder in a sign of pure love and contentment.

Again, Jasper growled at his brother and Willow ached that he was stuck with her. Dammit, she really needed to get over herself and show him that she was worth it. Maybe tomorrow.

She smiled and nodded at him. Words stopped in her throat and she found herself unable to speak again. For supposedly being such a smart person, she wasn't doing too hot at this moment.

Jasper squeezed the side of her hip and turned her to the scarred man the corner. "Maddox, this is my mate. Behave. Willow, this is Maddox. Pay no attention to him."

Maddox stood to his full height, which was about five inches shorter than Jasper's six foot six, and stuck his hands in his pockets as if he were afraid to touch her. He had dark blond hair, and other than the long scar that ran down the side of his right cheek from eye to chin, he looked familiar. She'd seen this face before. North.

"Twins." Her voice only a whisper, but the wolves heard.

"Yep." Maddox gave her a sad quirk of his lips. "But I am the pretty one." He sat back down without another word and folded his arms across his chest. Sadness slid across his eyes.

Why would he be sad?

"It's nice to meet all of you." Her voice finally returned but she was too overwhelmed meeting his family to say anything more.

"Don't forget me."

A sultry voice came from behind them, and Willow turned to see the most beautiful woman she'd ever laid eyes on. She was about five foot five and fit but skinny. She had a lighter version of Jasper's green eyes and straight black hair, that was so black it was almost blue.

"Now that you've met the brothers, I guess it's time to meet the sister." Jasper's sister glided across the room like a dancer and gave Willow a strong hug.

"It's good to have more women here. I can only take so much testosterone."

"Cailin, I was getting to it. You weren't here yet." Jasper gave his sister an exasperated look and nodded toward her. "Willow, this brat is my annoying baby sister Cailin. Beware, she may look nice now, but she bites." Jasper tossed them both a playful look before the room erupted with laughter.

"Dude, I would keep one eye open tonight. Cailin is likely to gut you for that remark." Someone – it sounded like Reed –warned Jasper.

"Let's take a seat, and ignore Reed." Jasper's face sobered before he continued. "We're here so I can tell you a little bit more about being a werewolf, what my family's Pack positions are and answer any other questions you may have."

Willow just nodded and urged Jasper to continue. This was one of the moments she'd been waiting for.

She was in a new place, filled with new people. Now, she has a new family, but knew nothing about them. The glimpse of a nice little life that could come her way if she stayed with Jasper would be nice. But she was still terrified.

She was Jasper's mate. Right? But he didn't really want

her. There were a million things to both dread and look forward to, but first she needed some answers. And at this moment, he was offering some. She had dozens of questions, but no idea where to start or stop. She needed to shut up and listen. Her mind spun and she blinked at Jasper's concerned face.

"Okay, werewolves can be born and made. Most wolves are born. Turning someone is beyond painful. It takes a bite and almost true death for it to occur. And even then, sometimes the change doesn't take, and they die anyway. Hence the reason we don't do it often."

She didn't know if she wanted to be a werewolf just yet, but a little pain wasn't going to keep her from him. Okay, he said a lot of pain. But that still couldn't stop her if she set her mind to it.

Jasper held her hand and goose bumps spread over her arms. Her body flared with a subtle arousal and she blushed. This overwhelming need for him shouldn't be happening so soon. But ever since that bite, she couldn't stop wanting him. Thinking about their future. Crazy, but real.

"Our wolves live within. They're another being we try to work cohesively with. However, at a young age, we must learn to take control over them. They're more primitive and in more tune with nature than our human selves. Unlike what the media portrays, we don't need the moon to shift, but during the full moon, our wolves are more of a presence, and we do feel the call toward it. At that time, our Pack likes to go for hunts as a group. The full moon pulls us together as a Pack and allows our wolves in control, if only for a short while."

"So all of you turn into wolves?" She asked.

Jasper smiled and a lock of hair fell into his eyes. Oh how she wanted to brush it out of his face. But she didn't want to come on too strong.

"Yes, all of us do."

"Can your wolves talk?"

"They talk to us in our heads." He grinned and she wanted to kiss him. "It's like having another person inside your head sometimes and gets annoying, but you get used to it."

"That's really weird. Do you talk out loud?"

He laughed, his brothers joining in. "Sometimes. But mostly we just respond in our heads."

"So your wolf is its own being."

"Yes, and much older than us. Like an old soul."

"Really?" How awesome was that?

"Really." He smiled and brushed her cheek with the back of his hand. Warmth tingled throughout her body and she struggled not to jump on his lap.

Where was this coming from?

"As for the positions in the Pack," Jasper continued. "It can be a little more complicated. What I am about to tell you goes no farther than this room. Not all in the Pack know every part of every position, and not all Packs have our, for lack of a better word, magic. But since you're my mate, you have the right to know all of this."

There was that word again. *Mate.*

"First there is the Alpha, the leader." Jasper continued. "Our father. The Alpha can feel every single one of his Pack's souls. Some bonds are stronger than others, like those with his family, but no matter what the relationship, he can feel them, and the Pack is comforted by that. Also as the Alpha, he leads the Pack and makes the decisions. We're not a democracy, and there's no council of elders who decides things. Our elders are our knowledge holders, not our masters. If the Alpha is corrupt, then someone can challenge for his seat, but it would take a strong wolf to take down our father. As it is, I am not sure anyone other than one of his sons could do it, and I don't think we would.

"The Alpha's sons hold most of the other positions. Only three are by birth, however. The others are gifts sent by the magic of the wolf that blesses them with their gifts." Maddox snorted at this statement, but Jasper ignored him. "Our generation, however, is the first to be missing one of the positions gifted to us, but that just means we haven't found that person yet.

"Back to the positions. The Alpha's first son is also an Alpha wolf in terms of his strength. He is called the Heir, and in our case that title falls to Kade. He too can feel the Pack, but not to the degree that our father can. As he ages and gets closer to taking over the Pack as true Alpha, the strength of the bond and his responsibilities with increase. Our father can either die to give Kade the new position or step down in the future when he reaches a certain age, but as Dad is only around two-hundred and fifty and Kade is only a hundred-and-five, he still has time."

Willow's jaw dropped, and Jasper smiled.

He looked damned sexy for his age.

But what if she didn't change? So she'd grow old and die while Jasper stayed young? A shiver crept through her. She couldn't live with that.

Jasper chuckled. "I guess I forgot to tell you. As werewolves, we age very slowly. We are not immortal, but we are harder to kill. I think the oldest wolf we have at the moment is about one thousand, but she is very secretive about her age. This is one of the reasons mates choose the change to werewolves. It would be a sad existence to watch your love grow old and frail and not be able to do anything about it."

No one spoke at that depressing thought. At that moment, Willow decided that, no matter what Jasper thought, she would change. She would be by his side and take care of him and be his mate. He may resent her, but she would take the lifetimes they had together to make it up to him.

"Right." Jasper cleared his throat before continuing. "Next in line is the second son, me. At a hundred and three, I'm the Beta of the Pack. I take care of the daily tedious duties around the Pack and my main job is to ensure our existence remains a secret. I will keep my job until Kade's second son comes of age and is prepared to take over. As Mel and Kade have only recently been mated and have no children, yet, I will be Beta for a while."

"But what about if Kade doesn't have a second son? Will you always be Beta?" She asked.

"If they don't have a second son, then I'll always be Beta. If I die, then the second son of the oldest Jamenson will be Beta. No matter what, the power will stay in our family line. We just have to hope that we have a lot of sons."

"That sounds a bit sexist."

Jasper laughed. "Believe me, I know. But I didn't make it up. Maybe as time change, fate will change the way the power forms. But so far the Jamensons have been, shall we say productive."

The others in the room laughed.

"What do you mean?"

"I mean that we all have many kids, so there usually isn't a problem."

"Oh." She felt a blush rise up in her cheeks.

This was all so much to take in. Power and hierarchy so different from her own. Her head hurt.

"The third son, Adam – who's one hundred– is the Enforcer. His job is inner Pack discipline and protecting the Pack from outside forces. Though we all do the latter, he is in charge of most of it daily. Thankfully Adam is one tough son of a bitch and is good at his job." Adam gave them both a half smile and shook his head.

"There's also the Omega. This position is not relegated to only the Alpha's family, however, Maddox was lucky enough to be called on."

This time Maddox didn't quirk his lips or snort.

"At ninety-six, he can feel all of the emotions of the Pack."

"But how is that different than the Alpha, Heir or you?"

"The rest of us can only feel that they are there. We don't know if they what they are feeling – emotionally or physically. But Maddox can feel *all* the emotions. Some stronger than others and he can never fully turn them off or ignore them. Touch seems to strengthen the bond so give him space. It's also his duty to the Pack to help with these emotions, but as anyone knows, help is sometimes not easy or welcome."

Maddox sat in his corner with a blank face and his arms folded against his chest. Only his eyes gave away the torture and emotions he must feel. Willow inwardly winced at the everything he must have been feeling.

"Maddox," she asked, "how can you stand all of it?"

"I have to." He answered. "All the happiness, pain, every type of emotion is multiplied. You get used to it." He shrugged and she didn't believe him.

Again the room grew silent before Jasper continued.

"Last is our Healer. Their job is to heal physical wounds.

They can fix most small wounds and, with only immense power, can heal stronger ones. Right now that place is vacant as our father lost his brothers in the last war. We are unsure why we don't have one, but I can only guess that someone will come to our Pack with the ability, maybe as one of our mates."

Well, she sure wasn't the healer. She could barely put on a Band-Aid.

"I thought North would be your Healer?" She asked.

"He's a medically trained doctor, but doesn't have the magic. And he can't feel the physical wounds that the Healer can."

Willow's eyes widened. "The Healer can feel *all* wounds?"

"Not the actual pain, but they can tell they're hurt."

"Those are the major Pack positions. But each of us do our parts. Mom is the Alpha female and aids Dad. She's unlike Alphas most that though in that she looks like a good little housewife, but she can eliminate threats with the best of us and helps make all of Dad's decisions. They're a fully functioning working pair."

He gave Mel a smile, "Mel is a chemist who has a job outside the den, but she's working on upgrading our archaic attitudes and helping around the Pack." The men all snorted. "But one day she will take over Mom's job, and I'm sure she is opinionated enough that Kade won't revert to the old ways." Mel laughed out loud and everyone in the room joined her.

Oh, she already liked Mel.

"Too true, man. Too true." Kade leaned in gave his mate a full-on-the-mouth kiss that seemed inappropriate outside the bedroom, but didn't seem to faze the wolves.

Willow shrugged. Apparently, wolves were a little more physical and open. As long as Jasper did the same to her, she would be just dandy with that. A blush crept up her cheeks and she lowered her eyes Maddox arched his eyebrow toward her.

Darn emotions. No hiding from wolves.

"Reed is ninety-eight, an artist, and draws our Pack history. He says he doesn't do much, but we need it, and it helps the cubs learn to shift. North, as you know, is our Pack doctor. Without him I don't know what our Pack would do."

Both brothers looked uncomfortable with Jasper's praise.

"And me, Jasper? What do I do?" Cailin's voice grew soft and seemed so sad.

"You, my dear sister, at twenty-three and the Alpha's only daughter, can be whatever you want to be."

Cailin snorted. "Seriously? I'm not even allowed out of the den. I'm stuck here as the 'precious princess'. No, thank you." She turned toward Willow. "I use herbs to make medicine for North and I also make music. But I *will* find a way to be useful to the Pack, rather than just falling into a good marriage because I have the ability to breed pups."

Pups? Yeah, Jasper needed to explain that one.

Jasper let out a small growl. "You will mate who you want, when you want. Dad's not like some of the other older wolves out there who see you for political gain."

Cailin didn't respond, but looked unconvinced.

Willow didn't envy her. Though the thought of having such a large family seemed amazing, the whole overprotectiveness thing was a bit much.

"Well then." Mel said, breaking the tension. "Kade and I made an early dinner. Let's eat and get to know Willow. Shall we?" Mel pulled Cailin to her feet and dragged her to the kitchen. The rest of them followed.

Jasper and Willow sat alone in the room, her thoughts going in a million directions.

"Thank you, Jasper."

"For what? Scaring you?"

"No, for telling me the truth. For not keeping secrets. I know we have a lot more to talk about but thank you for sharing with me what you did." Boldly she reached up and pressed her lips to his in a sweet kiss.

Willow could almost feel the future with this man, this wolf. Now she only needed to make sure he felt the same way.

7

———

Later that evening, her heart beating loudly in her ears, Willow clung to Jasper's hand as he led her to the Pack circle. The Alpha planned to introduce her to the Pack and discuss her kidnapping and its ramifications with the Central Pack. Located in a valley filled with tall trees and grass, the meeting place nestled between two rock faces. Raised edges formed stadium seating in the rock worn smooth over time, and Willow was surprised they actually were comfortable. In the center lay a flat grassy plane surrounded by mud and dirt, like an archaic football field. The pulse of Pack energy coming from the circle and the weight of boundless magic and decisions over centuries danced over her skin.

"So is everyone going to be in wolf or human form?" Willow asked.

Okay, that was a stupid question. But she hated silence.

Jasper laughed. "Human form. As much as we love our wolf ones, it's kinda hard to talk to each other on four feet."

Willow laughed. "Oh, but how do you communicate when you are a wolf?"

"Instinct. We follow each other or move our heads to indicate where we want to go. It isn't like we have philosophical discussions when we're hunting. I know some myths say we can talk telepathically, and though that would be cool as hell, we don't."

"So, no mind readers. Good to know."

"Well, not that I know of anyway. But it could happen I guess. Maybe it comes after mating." Jasper smiled.

"Really? What am I thinking now?" Willow teased.

"That I look good in this shirt?" Jasper laughed.

Willow widened her eyes. "Wow. I can't believe it. You caught me."

They laughed, and Jasper held her close to his side. "Really? I'll have to wear this more often."

He leaned down and brushed his lips on her hair. Heat radiated over her skin. Thank God he couldn't actually read her mind right now. She'd die of mortification.

As they stepped into the circle to sit with his family, Willow felt the eyes of dozens of wolves in human form home in on her and Jasper. Some looked wary of a new face; others were mildly curious. Some of the men stared at her appreciatively before inhaling deeply froze. Their eyes widened and their jaws dropped. She didn't know what that meant, but she burrowed into Jasper's side nonetheless. He let go of her hand and wrapped a possessive arm around her. Her rapid heartbeat immediately calmed as a feeling of peace swept over her.

When Jasper moved, the anger and disbelief from some of the women in the circle crawled over her skin. They glared, curling their lips, then scoffed. One woman snarled and looked at Willow as if she were a bug in need of being wiped from the windshield. Jasper's arm tightened around her, and he bent down to whisper in her ear.

His warm breath tickled her neck, and she shivered as he spoke. "That's Camille. She's let her desire to be my mate known, but she doesn't have the potential, nor does she make my wolf want her. Even if she did, she's too shrewd to be worth it. I will always protect you, but be wary of her. She's a bitch in every sense of the word." She felt his lips brush against her temple before he straightened and led them to their places.

People milled about until Edward took his place at the stone alter. His loud booming voice echoed throughout the circle, as if magic aided it.

"Settle, Pack."

With two words, the sounds of rustling and subtle chatter dissipated. The power of his voice as an Alpha swept over her, and a feeling of belonging settling in. Was it because of the mate mark? Or something more?

"We're here tonight for two purposes," Edward said. "To welcome our new Pack member, my son's mate, Willow Delton Jamenson." The new name startled her, and she looked at Jasper for a clue, but he merely shook his head and mouthed "Later."

"We are also here to discuss the reasons for which she's entered the Pack and what must be done to strengthen our resolve and protect our future."

The wolves murmured their welcome to her and some even smiled in her direction. She smiled back and tried not to look like an idiot with her still bruised and cut face. Jasper tightened his arm around her.

God, she was falling in love with this man! Tears welled in her eyes, but she held them back. She would not cry in front of his Pack.

"Jasper's mate will be an asset to our Pack, and I am truly honored to have her as part of our family." His normally harsh stare warmed when he turned toward her with a quirk of his lips. The warmth disappeared in a flash, as he turned again to address the circle.

"However, in order for her to join us, my sons had to rescue her first. The Central Pack kidnapped her from her place of business against her will." Edward's eyes glowed with anger as the tension level of the Pack members in the circle rose.

Chaos erupted as the Alpha relayed the events of her kidnapping. Wolves shouted and growled on her behalf.

Willow looked at the faces, angry and seething. Anger for her. She was touched. Their willingness to retaliate because of her mistreatment humbled her. When her gaze reached Camille, the woman had the nerve to smirk. She sighed.

Oh well, guess she couldn't please everyone.

"Settle down Pack." The growling stopped immediately when Edward's voice rose above the crowd. "My sons have already been back to the location, but found it empty. They have abandoned that part of the territory line but have violated our treaty by stepping foot on our land. We will find them and take them down, but we must protect our Pack!"

"Wait!" Willow's voice broke through the noise and all eyes turned to her. "Do we have to attack right away? I mean can't we make sure everyone else is safe first?" She plopped down next to Jasper and rubbed her forehead.

Stupid! Why did she have to say anything?

"Yeah? Why risk our Pack for her?" Camille said, the words spewing from her mouth like raw sewage.

Willow's belly tightened with knots. This woman scared her.

"You will watch your tongue, Camille, before I take it from you," Jasper growled. His eyes glowed to a bright gold, blazing in his anger.

Camille immediately lowered her gaze, but still had a smirk on her face.

"Willow, we will protect the Pack, but these cruelties

cannot go unchallenged. We are a strong Pack, and we protect our own." Edward's voice signaled the end of that line of the conversation, and he continued to discuss how they would retaliate.

Flushed with embarrassment, Willow sat silent for the rest of the meeting, wondering what Jasper thought of her after that little outburst. She really had to try harder at keeping her mouth shut.

Jasper leaned over and whispered, "It's okay, Willow, you just don't know Pack protocol yet. It takes time, but I will always fight for you. No matter what." He kissed her temple and pulled her firmly against him.

When the meeting ended, Jasper led her back to his house. Something crunched on the gravel, and Willow paused.

When she looked up, she saw the man who'd given her that lewd look in the Circle. Geez, he gave her the creeps. He smiled at her, and she fought the urge to vomit.

"Franklin, remove yourself from our path. I don't have the patience for you tonight." Jasper's voice cooled, and he moved her behind him.

"*Tsk tsk,* Jasper. You missed something, didn't you? I only saw the mark against her shoulder, but the mating isn't complete, is it? What, couldn't take her for a ride yet? Your cock broken?"

Willow didn't even see Jasper move before his fist

connected with Franklin's face and the other wolf was on the ground.

"Poor move, Beta. You need to finish that bitch, or I'll take her. Watch your back."

Jasper ignored him and picked Willow up and carried her to his home. Movement over his shoulder drew her gaze to Adam and Maddox carelessly lifting Franklin and leading him back to the circle.

He set her down in the foyer while he closed the door behind him.

"Jasper? What did he mean the mating wasn't complete? What's going on?" Her heart beat faster.

This was all too much. Did he have to bite her again? Mate her in public or something? Like in those romance novels? She hardly knew him, but she didn't want to lose him.

"He meant we've only completed part of the mating. I have to spill my seed in your womb to bind our human halves. The mate mark only claims you as my wolf's mate." Jasper's face darkened and he looked angry at the prospect.

"Oh." What else was there to say? His wolf and the situation had forced him into biting her. Now he didn't want to finish claiming her? He didn't want to make love to her. Coldness crept from her heart into her veins. The loss for something she hadn't even known she craved ached in her chest. For all her affirming and promising she would make Jasper see she was worth it, he deliberately held more of himself back to prove he didn't want her. It hurt.

Willow had been thrown from home to home her whole life. She had no family and meeting the Jamensons had already brightened her life. No stupid mating rule could tear her away. Not now. She straightened her shoulders and prayed she didn't make a fool of herself.

"Well then. I guess we can change that can't we?" She looked up into his deep green eyes. Heat radiated from him, warming her body in an intimate caress.

"You want to finish the mating?" Jasper's voice deepened to an animalistic growl. His nostrils flared as he took deep breaths.

"Please," she whispered.

He took the space between them in two steps and crushed his mouth to hers.

8

The flavor of his mate's mouth was a masterpiece of sugar and heat exploding on his taste buds. Jasper delved his tongue into Willow's mouth hard and fast, teeth clashing against teeth. He held her face in his hands, then held her hair back in a firm grip. Lifting his lips from hers, he framed the side of her face with his other hand, careful of her bruises.

"You're so beautiful." His words were a whispered growl that sent shivers down his mate's slender body.

The wolf inside him prowled and preened, eager to finish the mating and mount to completion. The man wanted to fuck her hard against the wall and then twice more against the counter and bed just because he could. But first he had to shake away the doubt he'd seen clouding her eyes throughout the day.

"Willow, I chose you. Do you understand that? I came to you and asked you to be with me. If not for them taking you from me, I still would have chosen you. I choose you." He held her against him, pleading with his eyes and baring his soul.

Willow's eyes widened but before she could speak, Jasper kissed her again, a soft caress against her lips.

"I know you didn't ask for this, but I will do everything in my power as a man, as Beta of this Pack, as your mate, to be worthy of you. I never want to see the fear and pain in your eyes again. I want to see the light and sweetness that I have begun to fall in love with every day for the rest of my days." Jasper's heartbeat reverberated in his ears, and he and his wolf waited for her response. He could feel Willow's pulse quicken underneath his fingertips as they rested on her silky skin.

He watched as her throat worked as she tried to speak. "I thought..." She hiccupped a sob and Jasper's grip tightened, "I thought you were forced." She swallowed hard, and tears spilled down her cheeks. "I already promised myself I would do what I could to be worthy of you." Jasper kissed her tears as she sobbed, trailing them to her lips in a hard and demanding kiss.

They both stepped back and took a deep breath.

"It's me who's not worthy of you," he rasped.

"I choose you, too," she whispered.

At her words, his wolf howled in approval as he took her

sweet ass in his hands and lifted her against the wall. Her eyes closed, and her dark lashes lay against her milky white skin intensifying her beauty. Kneading her ass, he kissed her again, running his tongue against the seam of her lips, reveling in the softness of them. Moving from her mouth, he nibbled her chin and licked and suckled her neck to behind her ear. She shivered as her heat ground against his rigid length.

Growling, he bit harder on her mate mark and watched the shock of ecstasy wash across her face. He'd heard the mark was an erogenous zone and filed that tid bit of knowledge for later. Lifting his face from her neck as her hand roamed his body, he searched for a place to take her.

"I'm going to fuck you hard and fast this first time, then I'm going to take you nice and slow so I can savor you." Her answering moan and shudder was the only response he needed.

When they'd first came home, they entered the house through the garage and the nearest flat surface was his woodworking table. That would have to do.

Carrying her with her legs wrapped around his, while still kissing and kneading her, proved more difficult than he would have imagined. For his advanced age, he acted like a pup. If she didn't stop rubbing against his cock like that, he was gonna blow in his pants before he even got to feel her heat wrapped around him.

Still holding her with one arm, he used the other to

viciously swipe away the odds and ends on the table. A loud crashing sound echoed in the room, followed by Willow's giggle. He bit into her plump lip.

"You think that's funny, do you? Am I going to have to punish you for making fun of me?" He smiled to show he was only joking. Her pupils dilated with arousal, and he growled in approval. Laying her on the table like a pagan sacrifice, he admired her hair spread like a chestnut halo about her head. Her cheeks blushed and her eyes bright, she'd never looked sexier.

He removed her shoes and swept his hands up her legs slowly, stopping every so often to squeeze and rub. Her breath quickened, and his heart pounded. He trailed his fingers along her inner thigh, purposely missing her core. She moaned. And when he reached her button fly, she held her breath. His wolf tried to claw to the surface, too eager to care about control, but Jasper held back. He wanted to take his time and make her feel comfortable. To feel loved.

He popped each button on her fly, released her jeans from her waist, and slid them down her legs. He froze.

Damn. She wasn't wearing any underwear.

Fuck. Him.

Blushing furiously, Willow tried to cover herself, but he stopped grabbed her wrist and held it above her head.

"I didn't have any clean, and that isn't something you can borrow, you know?" She looked so innocent, and he wanted to eat her up. Everywhere.

"I would say that's something I have to fix, but I like you bare. Tomorrow, though, I'll get you anything you need. I promise, but right now… Damn, I love your pussy."

Light brown curls, slightly groomed, covered her mound. Jasper growled with lust. He didn't want a little girl with just skin. He wanted a woman who could produce his pups and take all of his cock.

Tracing his fingers around her outer lips, he followed the trail of curls to her center. He dipped one finger to the knuckle. Wet heat clenched around him. Damn. He removed his finger and licked it.

Jesus. She tasted of cinnamon and sugar everywhere. He sat her up and ripped off her shirt and stiffened at her naked breasts. Put new bra on the shopping list. Her nipples hardened under his gaze.

Scratch that. No bra. Ever.

Dusky pink nipples puckered in the cold air of his work room. Small breasts that could easily fit in his hands. He sucked on her lips again because he couldn't resist her taste and trailed down her neck to her nipples. He latched on to her right breast where he sucked and bit until she thrashed against him. He brushed his fingers down her stomach, and he thrust two fingers hard and fast into her. Gasping, she came against his hand at the first thrust and screamed his name.

Jasper released her breast and licked her collar bone.

"That's it, Willow. Ride it, baby." He crooked his fingers to ride on her G-spot as she rode the wave of her orgasm.

As she lay boneless on the table, Jasper quickly removed his clothes and lifted her legs to his shoulders. Damn, he loved a flexible woman. His Willow was perfect for him. He brushed her clit with his tip.

"Watch me, Willow. Watch me take you. Feel my cock fill you, then feel my seed as our souls merge." Too entranced to find words, she merely nodded. He gripped her waist to secure her to the table and entered her to the hilt in one thrust. She screamed, and he froze.

"Wil? Did I hurt you? Am I too rough? You're just so tight. I don't want to hurt you." Though it ached not to move, he knew she was still tender from her orgasm.

His mate shook her head before answering. "No. No. It feels so good, Jasper. It's just been so long, and you're so big."

Jasper chuckled. "Well, we could have worse problems, I guess. Are you ready for me to move?"

At her nod, he swiftly withdrew before slamming back home. Her breasts jiggled with the force. He did it again and again, each time aiming deeper until she was almost convulsing around him. Her wet heat was so tight around his cock that, when his balls drew up, he knew he wouldn't last much longer. He flicked her clit until her eyes glassed over and her body shuddered in release.

He howled as his seed spilled into her womb and he felt

the final mating bond lock into place. Willow's soul and happiness wrapped around his in a tight and loving embrace. A look of awe crossed her face.

Thank God he wasn't the only one feeling this.

He'd thought he'd known what mating meant, but now he realized he didn't have a damn clue. It was so much more than saying they were bound. Her very essence flowed within him, her love for him radiating from every pore. Still inside her, he leaned over her, and wrapped his arms around her body, refusing to relinquish the connection.

"I can feel you," Willows whispered. Tears fell to down her cheeks, and he kissed her softly on the lips, pouring all his love into that one kiss.

"I can feel you too. I love you. Willow."

Sighing, she kissed him fully back. "I love you too, Jasper."

Tears fell to her shoulder, and he knew they must be his. The Beta of the Redwood Pack, the fiercest Pack of them all, was crying about his mate and he didn't feel at all bad about it.

9

It was time. They gathered in North's basement, nervous with fear and anticipation. The harsh sterile smell of a medical room attacked his wolf senses, heightening the tension in the room. White walls, bare of personal touches, closed in like prison bars.

Tonight Melanie was officially becoming part of the Pack. She'd become a werewolf. It would be a brutal process that required near death. Though Jasper had helped in many changes throughout his years, he didn't know if he could stomach this particular one. Since meeting her, Melanie had become a sister to him. Watching her go through the change might take a part of his soul with her.

Looking at his mate, his heart clenched. Her chestnut hair was pulled back from her face, enhancing her soft beauty. Willow desired to be changed as well, but would she after witnessing this? That morning he'd woken up wrapped around his warm mate. The feel of her heart beat against his chest in sync with his own made both the wolf and the man want to howl for joy. She and he were tired from their initial mating and then twice more in the middle of the night.

His wolf brushed the surface of his mind. *"It was about time we mated her. I can feel her soul with ours. Once she is changed I know she will be a beautiful wolf."*

He could only agree with his wolf. But he fought the very idea. All of the happiness that Jasper had gained from Willow the night before sucked from him like a vacuum. Scared beyond what he liked to admit, he tried to prepare himself for what was to come.

Muscles aching from their hard and fast gymnastics the night before, Jasper stretched his body before coming to Kade's side. His brother bent over Melanie, whispering reassurances and words of peace in her ear, though from the looks of it, Melanie was the calmer of the two.

Strapped down to a table with cords and wires covering her to take her vitals, she looked nervous, but at an odd form of peace. Her chest moved with her deep breaths and Kade rubbed her arms and stomach before placing a gentle kiss on her lips. Jasper could hear a faintly whispered "I love you" before Kade backed away from her.

"Mel, I know this will hurt, but we can't give you drugs. It'll interfere with the change and may cause adverse reactions." North's voice was calm, though he didn't mention the actual reactions, as those were too grotesque.

Pulling Kade back to the corner of the room, Jasper took a good look at his family. Though not all of them were needed for the change to take place, they came to show support for both Melanie and Kade in their time of need. He truly loved his family.

Willow stood behind Mel's head, holding her hand and wiping her brow. As if she could feel him looking at her, she looked up into his eyes, giving him a small smile. Heart aching for her, he smiled back. Maddox stood beside her, holding Mel's other hand, murmuring comforting words, using his gift to calm her emotions.

Reed, Adam, and he held Kade back in a corner. The bite and mauling of his mate to induce the change would be painful for not only her but would cause Kade's wolf to go ballistic and want to kill anyone who would hurt his mate. With as much power that ran in Kade's veins, it would take the three of them to hold him back when he and his wolf were enraged. They asked Kade to back out of the room, knowing full well it was a lost cause. Kade refused to part with his mate. If things went wrong, he needed to be near her.

Again Jasper thought of Willow and the fact she'd

expressed interest in changing. Though their lifetimes varied dramatically, he didn't know if he could risk her dying now rather than dying in only a few short decades. A hurdle to be jumped later.

Cailin and his mom were aiding North with his medical preparations and would act as nurses if the need arose.

The clicking of claws on the linoleum brought silence to the room. A large and magnificent gray wolf entered. The sight of his father in his wolf form always urged Jasper to bow his head. Though Jasper was a strong wolf, the immense power and pride emanating from their Alpha was a force to be respected.

Putting one paw in front of another, his father prowled farther in the room. Jasper watched as Mel's eyes widened before she continued taking shallow breaths. Kade growled and whimpered while pushing at the three holding him back.

"Shh, it will be over soon." Jasper's whispered words were empty placations even to his own ears.

Before he could blink, his father charged and pounced on the table. Teeth pierced Mel's shoulder, the shoulder opposite Kade's mate mark. Kade's wolf came to the surface, claws erupting from his fingertips. His brother tried to claw and bite his way through the barrier of strong werewolves. Jasper planted his feet and held on to him with his gaze still on Mel and Wil.

Mel screamed in agony but kept her attention on

Willow. The bite in her shoulder was not that of a mate mark, but a brutal assault that forced the change by adding the enzyme to her blood. For the greatest chance of a conversion occurring, the Alpha had to be the one to bring her over. His father released Mel's shoulder only to bite and tear into the flesh of her chest and stomach. Blood seeped into the crisp white sheets she lay across, a crimson splash of color against the stark contrast of sterility. Ripping into her side with his teeth and claws, his father continued to bring Mel near death. Her body convulsed and thrashed, fighting the chains and ropes holding her down. She screamed and cried, the sound piercing his heart, before finally passing out from the pain. Still, his father didn't quit, for she needed to be as close to death as possible to ensure the change, one bite wasn't enough.

Tears running down his cheeks, Kade screamed and growled, putting his full Heir's powers into fighting his brothers to get to his mate. Adam pulled his arm back and punched Kade directly in the face, crashing his head into the wall. Reed bent down and shouldered him in the stomach with a grunt, keeping him pinned. Jasper put his elbow against Kade's throat and the other across his chest. However much pain the brothers inflicted on him, Jasper knew the pain from seeing his mate in distress and practically dying in front of him would be worse.

Jasper looked across the room at Maddox and blink. His younger brother paled to a deathly white. His teeth digging into his lip, cutting into the flesh. He shook, his hand still gripping Mel's as he took her pain.

How the hell did he do it?

Finally, after what felt like hours later, his father backed from Melanie's seemingly lifeless body before changing back into a man. His mother quickly left her daughter-in-law's side and put a robe around her pale husband. For all the Alpha in his father, he still looked shaken. It must have been agony for his father to inflict his son's mate with that type of pain. Jasper didn't envy him.

Things moved quickly. North and Cailin expertly took Mel's vitals before cleaning her and wrapping her in cool cloth infused with herbs that would aide in healing her wounds. All the while, Willow and Maddox continued to hold Mel's hands and whisper to her motionless body.

He prayed the change took. Prayed another old soul and spirit of a wolf found its way into Mel's body and blended together in perfect harmony. The enzyme may force the change to start – but it took a magic power beyond their touch for it to stay.

Jasper looked around the room and froze. Every single person wept. The strongest family of wolves in the known world broke down, weeping for their own. The salty taste of his own tears reminded him of the night before when Willow and he had finally mated. The memory proved to be bitter sweet at this drastic difference in situation.

Watching the pain and sorrow in his mate's face he

knew he couldn't let her change. Though he would love to live his long life with her, he didn't know if he could see her harmed as Melanie had been. Taking a deep breath while still holding his brother back, he vowed that he would do all in his power to keep her from changing.

Once Melanie's vitals calmed, Kade did as well. Pushing past his brothers, he knelt at his unconscious mate's side and wept. Praying the change had taken hold, the family silently left room to give the pair a moment of peace.

As soon as they were upstairs, Willow rushed into Jasper's arms, clinging to him for support. With only a nod to his brothers, he picked up his mate and carried her home so that they could try to remember that they were alive and possessed each other.

WILLOW RUBBED her nose against Jasper's neck, inhaling his woodsy wolf and man scent. He smelled like home. Curling into his body, she let herself relax. Though she tried to be stoic and strong for Melanie, she'd been as frightened as when the Central Pack had taken her. Watching Edward tear into her new friend's body had taken all of Willow's inner strength not to run from the room. Knowing Jasper was there to cling to later was the only thing that kept her calm.

Jasper didn't let her go as they entered his, no their,

home. Closing the door behind him he strode toward the bedroom and set her feet on the floor while dragging his hands up the sides of her body to cradle her face.

"I love you, baby. I don't think I can live without you." Warm breath tickled her lips as he whispered his devotion.

"I love you, too." Her heart ached for him, and she needed him inside her – now.

He brushed his lips softly against hers. Jasper dropped his hands from her face and gently pushed her down until she lay on the bed. He took off her leggings and top leaving her bare before him. Willow's breath hitched. His pupils grew until only a small rim of forest green remained, a ring of gold glowed around the green. Kneeling before her, he took her legs and spread them so she was completely open to his gaze. The corner of his mouth quirked when he looked at her pussy. His nostrils flared, taking in her scent.

"I haven't even touched you yet and you're already glistening for me." His voice lowered, rough as if it was hard for him to speak. Taking her knees in his hands, he abruptly pulled her toward him so her ass lay at the edge of the bed and her cunt directly in his face. He gave a wicked smile before leaning over and licking her from puckered hole to the top of her mound with his wide tongue. Her hips bucked from the bed, but he quickly placed his palms on her pelvic bone to keep her secure. Looking up at her, he licked the juices from his lips, and his eyes glowed gold.

Before she could gain the energy to speak, he suckled

her clit. Rubbing her mound against his nose, she moaned and tried to twist her body. It was too much; he sucked and sucked while moving his tongue quickly against her clit. He trailed one palm down to cup her ass as he squeezed the globe and growled against her pussy. The rumbling of his growl caused her clit to tingle and her pussy to clench. Removing the hand from her ass, he took two fingers and circled her opening before entering her quickly. Curling his fingers, he rubbed her G-spot at the same time he bit down on her clit. Stars shattered behind her eyelids as she screamed his name until her throat was raw.

Even as she began to come down from her high, Jasper didn't relent. Rubbing her from the inside out and kissing her sweet center, he forced her to her peak again before she cascaded down.

"Oh my God." Her voice deepened with lust, her throat sore from screaming. *He is going to kill me with pleasure.*

"Call me Jasper." He laughed against her thighs at his lame joke before crawling up her body to lie next to her. Palming her breast in his rough hand, he tweaked her nipple, making her moan again.

"No more, baby. I need a moment." An idea came to her, and she gave him a sultry smile. "Don't move." He gave her a curious look but remained where he was.

As quickly as she could, she scooted down so she knelt on the bed between his legs. Raising an eyebrow in her direction, he knit his fingers behind his head and laid back as if he knew what she was about to do.

His cock was long and wide, with a slight curve to the right. That explained why he'd hit all of the perfect spots last night. *And it's all mine.* Giggling to herself, she took his cock in her hand and pumped it twice to watch the drop of pre-cum bead on the tip. Smiling again, she leaned down and licked it up. It tasted salty, yet sweet and still full of Jasper's forest taste.

Before he could stop her, she opened her mouth wide and relaxed her throat to take him fully into her mouth. When her lips reached the coarse hair at the base, she swallowed, allowing the back of the throat to squeeze the tip of his cock.

"Fuck! I didn't know you could do that! Fuck!" Out of the corner of her eyes, she saw one of his hands fisted in the comforter, and the other grabbed her hair in a tight almost painful grip. She made him fight for control. Nice. Moving back up his cock, she rolled her tongue until she released him with an audible pop.

Willow did this over and over again while rolling his balls in her palm before he gripped her hair tighter and pulled her off him.

"Damn, I was about to blow down your throat. It's too much." He panted and looked pained, his face strained. He gripped her hips and flipped their positions, digging her into the bed.

"But that was what I wanted to do." She stuck out her lower lip and pouted.

"But I want to come in your sweet pussy ,baby, with you wrapped around me."

Oh. When he put it that way…

Shivers danced down her spine, and she reached up to kiss him.

He knelt above her, their fingers entwined, before looking directly in her eyes. Slowing without blinking, he entered her. It was the perfect moment. Poignant and full of love. She could hear the catch in his breath and knew he would love her forever.

Slowly, he slid into her with two soft thrusts before slowly exiting her warmth then slamming back into her. He repeated this over and over until she was panting and moaning and begging for release, but they never broke eye contact.

Finally they groaned and came together before collapsing in a heap of tangled arms and sweat. Jasper leaned over and kissed her, murmuring his love before falling into a deep sleep. It had been an emotional day. That was for sure.

Willow, still encased in his arms, stayed awake a bit longer. The look of determination on his face after Melanie's attempt at the conversion had not been lost on her. He wasn't going to let her change. She was sure of it. Closing her eyes, she prayed for guidance, knowing the pain would be terrible, but the outcome of forever with Jasper would be worth it. She would do anything for him and to be with him. Whatever it took, she would be a werewolf. Be his werewolf. She would be a Jamenson in truth. Now she would have to convince Jasper. *No problem there.*

10

Incorporating one's self into a Pack of werewolves should come easy to anyone. Right? A snort escaped Willow before she could stop it. Though she had a leg up on others in meeting new people because of her past, she still was at a loss in some respects.

Her parents had died in a car crash when she was a little girl. She'd been sleeping in the back seat when a drunk driver hit them head on. Willow could still smell the scent of burned hair and blood. Could still hear the crunch of metal against metal. She could barely remember what they looked like.

Jasper helped alleviate that. His face and touch sent her to her dreams at night.

But what did she have to give back? Was she even worth it?

A twenty-four-year-old college dropout, she possessed little options in providing a true help to the Pack. She'd been relegated to being surrounded by a protection detail that would keep her from outside harm while Jasper's keen eye was elsewhere. Willow was learning the art of being a Pack member. Laughter rumbled in her chest at the irony.

"What's so funny?" Reed, her new brother-in-law, current bodyguard, and Pack artist asked. With a paintbrush in his hand, another brush behind his ear, and numerous splotches of colors from his current project, he looked like the typical struggling artisan. Lanky, with the build of a swimmer, his body held power and strength to fight any attack, though, anyone who faced him might laugh at the red smear on the tip of his nose.

"Nothing, just thinking. Here, let me get that." She reached for a clean towel behind him before rubbing his nose with it. They both collapsed in laughter as the red merely spread across his face and the towel.

"Great job, Wil. Before I may have looked like Rudolph; now I look like a clown bent on revenge." Gasping for breath, Willow dampened the cloth with more water, but Reed held her wrist.

"Please stop before I fully resemble a tomato." He took the towel from her hands and wiped his face the best he could. Honestly, it may have been too late for the tomato. She laughed again.

God, it felt so good to be with people who considered her family, even if they'd only known her for a short while. After surviving the car accident that took the lives of her parents at the age of six, Willow had bounced from foster home to foster home until she finally graduated high school. With the lack of connections to the human world, Reed and Adam told her she was a perfect candidate for entering the Pack, though, according to Jasper, that had no bearing on their mating. Either way, the warmth seeping through their mating bond shook off any doubt of his choice.

Thoughts and questions assailed her, and she didn't know whom to ask, but Reed seemed the most open.

"Can I ask you something, Reed?" Willow bit into her lip.

"Sure, Wil, what's up?" Reed cocked his head. He'd cleaned most of the red from his face, but a pink hue remained on his skin.

"Well, I would ask Jasper, but I don't want him to get the wrong idea. I mean, I love him, it's just..." She hung her head. Damn, this was harder to put into words than she'd thought. She stepped back, and her legs hit a stool, forcing her to take a seat.

"Now you're starting to worry me. Tell me what's going on." Reed knelt in front of her, taking her hand in his. Though he didn't possess the emotional magic Maddox did, nor the bond she shared with Jasper, Reed's touch cemented her in the present and gave her the courage to ask.

"Tell me about mating." The words tumbled from her mouth before she lost the nerve. "I know Jasper is my mate; I feel it here." She laid her hand on her heart, the beat pressing into her palm reminding her she was alive and connected to Jasper. "But I don't understand why others say Jasper had a choice. What don't I know?" Pain radiated through her chest at the thought of losing Jasper. That couldn't happen.

Reed furrowed his brow. "Jasper didn't explain it to you?" He shook his head. "I don't think I'm the right person to tell you. That is something between you and Jasper."

She gripped his hand harder, a lifeline to the unknown. "If I ask him, he'll think I question our bond, that I don't want him. That isn't how I feel, but I don't know anything about the Pack." Frustrated, she ground her teeth. "Just tell me. I won't leave him. I can't leave him. But I need to know." Her brother-in-law let out a breath. "Fine. But if Jasper tries to kick my ass, I blame you." A slight quirk of his lips softened his threat.

"Fate decides who's our perfect companion, who can connect our souls and complete our future. However, with the lifespan of a werewolf, fate's been kind. There are people out there with the potential to be our mate. We need only find them and mate them."

There were others? What she shared with Jasper wasn't unique? He could have another mate? Her heart clenched as thoughts swirled her mind, leaving her nauseated.

"Stop that, Willow. That's not what I meant. Jasper chose you. You are the ideal mate for him. Anyone else he could've mated wouldn't be perfect."

She shook her heat vigorously. "No, he didn't choose me. He was forced into it. Don't you understand?" Fear crept up her spine and she blinked away tears. Reed griped her chin, forcing her gaze back to his.

"Look at me. Jasper chose you. He chose you the moment he walked into your bakery all those months ago. He just wanted to take things slow. You can blame him for going at a snail's pace if you'd like." Reed gave a small laugh before continuing. "Just because fate allows us the option of different mates, it is truly difficult to find the one perfect mate. Jasper and you are mates. He marked you so cannot choose another while you live. And frankly, why would he? I see the way you two look at each other. And, Willow, honey, remember that we can hear great distances. Your home isn't exactly sound proof." A wicked smile crossed his lips as heat scalded her cheeks.

"Oh." Yeah, that sounded intelligent. She wrote a mental note to ask Jasper for some heavy drapes to dampen the sound from their bedroom. And their living room. And the kitchen...

"At least we know you two completed, right?" Reed laughed at his own joke as mortification set in. The Jamensons were a little too close for comfort sometimes.

"But I haven't marked him. What does that mean?"

Reed frowned. "That means you could leave him if you wanted. It would hurt the both of you like hell, but it could happen."

Oh.

"But I would never do that."

His face softened. "I know that, Wil."

"But seriously, Jasper and you are two halves of a whole. Believe me. Did Jasper tell you about Kade?" Her face must have revealed her confusion because Reed continued. "Before Kade met Melanie, he'd found another potential mate in Tracy. His wolf felt an ability to connect with her, and because she was a werewolf, he thought she would be a decent choice. However, Kade wasn't the only one who felt a connection to Tracy."

Reed shook his head and took a deep breath. "His best friend, Grant, sensed it too." Anger flashed across his face and he stopped talking.

Bewilderment settled in. Every time she spoke with a Pack member she learned something that blew away her expectations of normal.

"Two mates? What did Tracy do?" she asked.

"Tracy wanted them both and refused to choose, forcing Kade and Grant to fight for the right to mate her."

Alarm traveled up her spine. "What do you mean fight for her?" No way. Fighting like cavemen for a woman?

"They fought in the circle as men. Fist against fist. Flesh against flesh. But Kade's heart wasn't in it, so he conceded." With a shrug, Reed looked as if he didn't care Tracy wasn't his sister-in-law.

"But that's barbaric!"

"Willow, we aren't human. We're werewolves." He lifted an eyebrow. "You have taken everything we have thrown at you amazingly well, but is that because you still don't believe?" Concern was evident on his face with something else. Pity?

"I'm trying, Reed." Frustration engulfed her. Dammit, this was so new to her, wasn't she allowed a moment to be unsure?

"Don't feel sorry for Kade. It was because of the whole incident he met Melanie. After the circle he needed a night to himself, so we set him up on a blind date. As fate would have it, Melanie was his date and his mate." Reed laughed at his rhyme.

Willow rolled her eyes. Gah, even concerning serious topics, men could still act like they were twelve.

"So it worked out for Kade because there was a backup for him? Is it always like that?" The woman from the circle came to her mind – Camille. Willow pushed away jealous thoughts. Jasper was hers.

Again, Reed's face was so open the sorrow that swept his

face broke her heart. "Not always. Not for Adam. Not for Anna." The sound of the woman's name across his lips brought an ache to her chest, though she couldn't place why.

Reed took a steadying breath before continuing. "Adam was on a hunt when Anna was taken from their home. Before we could find her, she'd been raped and beaten. She was also pregnant with their first young." Tears ran down his cheeks, and Reed's voice broke. Poor Anna. Poor Adam.

"Maddox is the Omega, Willow. He could feel every painful blow Anna felt. Everything done to her, and been helpless to stop it. By the time we could get to her, Maddox was in a catatonic shock. There was nothing we could do. She was gone." Reed choked on his words. "There was no back up for him. He still feels her loss. We all do."

She couldn't take it anymore. Willow opened her arms and held Reed. This was Pack. Comforting one another, staying strong. This was something she could do.

Reed kissed the top of her head and stepped back. "Jasper would kill me if he came in and saw me in your arms. I happen to value my life." Their laughed quickly dissipated the tension.

"You are going to make some woman very happy one day Reed." His open heart and good nature would be a gift to anyone.

"Or man." He winked as Willow stared in shock.

"Man?" Well, that was unexpected.

"I'm open to either – or both. As long as there is a bond I'm happy." Reed smiled.

Huh, that was a nice way to look at it.

"Well then, good for you." They laughed together again as Reed picked up his forgotten paintbrush.

11

───────

W illow finally settled into life at the den. Being pulled forcefully from her normal routine and thrust into the world of the paranormal seemed to work for her. When the Central Pack abducted her, the bakery had been destroyed beyond repair. When they first saw the damage, they'd thought it was merely a few chairs and decorations. But Reggie and Isaac were thorough.

Bastards.

Her ovens and stoneware, gone or broken. Everything wasted. Willow's heart clenched at her broken dream. It wasn't fair. What had she done to deserve this? Everything she'd worked for was gone.

Jasper's response to the destruction was simple. Start fresh. They would use this horrible event to combine their lives and build together. Willow may have lost part of her life with the loss of her bakery, but her mate incorporated her into his life. That was more important than a few lost cinnamon rolls.

As it was, her talents in the kitchen weren't going to waste. Every morning she'd cook for him and her various new family members who "accidentally" showed up unexpectantly. That was something she was getting used to. Nothing like being bent over their kitchen table with a good morning from Jasper as a hungry werewolf walks through the door. Talk about embarrassing.

Her bakery might be closed but not her desire to feed people. It was amazing how well Jasper knew her after only such a short time. The center of the Den housed many small shops and provided goods for the needs and wants of the Pack. But there wasn't a place to eat that didn't involve going to someone's home. Here Willow could find her place, though she wasn't a werewolf – yet.

No matter how successful she'd thought she was before, the love radiating from Jasper and his family truly made her happy.

Willow took a deep breath and inhaled the mountain air. The crisp scent tugged at her heart and invigorated her bones.

"I love the air here. I mean I know it's only like twelve miles or so from where I lived before, but it just seems so much cleaner here." She breathed again and closed her eyes.

"I think you are sensing the magic in our air."

Willow opened her eyes at Reed's statement.

"Huh?" In the circle she'd thought she'd felt something, but smelling magic? That was a bit too weird for her.

"We're high up in the mountains in the most beautiful forest in the Americas, if not the world, so yes, the air is clean. But what makes it cling to your soul is the Pack magic inherent in everything we do. I know you aren't a werewolf, but you're connected through your bond with Jasper. You will be a little more open to feeling these things than an average human." Reed smiled and led her to a vacant building.

A familiar warmth spread though her heart and she smiled at the gorgeous specimen of man walking toward her.

"Jasper." His name was a reverent whisper. She couldn't help it.

Before she knew what she was doing, the smell of forest and mate surrounded her as she ran to him and Jasper clutched her tightly to his chest. His heart beat soundly against her cheek. Home.

"Mmm, it has been too long since I have seen you, my Willow." His lips were a light brush of sensual taste against hers.

"It's only been since this morning, Jasper." Smiling, she took his parted lips as an invitation, melding her tongue to his.

A discreet cough behind them reminded her of Reed's presence.

"Not that that wasn't hot, but really, I thought we came here for a reason." Reed's smile belied his sarcasm.

"Guess we did. Come, let me show you." Jasper kissed her brow and took her hand.

He grinned mischievously, and she smiled. He was up to something. What could he be planning with an old abandoned building?

"Jasper? It's an empty building. I mean, it's a nice one, but what are we doing here?"

"I know you've been putting on a brave face with losing your bakery. Wil, baby, that place was your dream. The product of your hard work and love. I know I can never replace that for you, but I can help us move on together. "This place? It's yours." Jasper opened his arms pointing to the barren walls and open space.

"What?" Her pulse quickened. Hers?

"Wil, you've been cooking and baking for Pack members for the four weeks you've been here and asked for nothing in return. The Pack and I recognize your passion for what you do, and we want to show you how much we love you. Open a bakery here, or do what you want with it. I know you want to contribute, and this is how you can do it. The Pack wants you – I want you." Jasper's jade eyes begged her to take the chance, to be part of his Pack in more than name.

"Mine? I mean..." She choked on a sob as the rush of

love and acceptance swept through her. They wanted her. They respected what she had to offer.

"Yours."

"Oh, Jasper, I love you. Thank you." She jumped into his arms and wrapped her legs around his waist.

"Still here, guys." Reed's voice startled her as Jasper laughed. "But really, Willow, we all want you to feel like you belong. And once you decide exactly what you are going to do, let me know. These grey and lonely walls are begging for a mural and my hands are itching to comply."

Again, her heart almost burst with joy and love as she slid down Jasper's body to plant her feet.

"What a pretty picture. The lovebirds and the twink." A vicious snarl and cruel words brought their celebration to a screeching halt. Camille. God, that woman was a bitch in every sense of the word. Beside the female wolf, Fredrick glared like the bully he was. Ever since the circle, those two had been inseparable and, frankly, annoying as hell. They just couldn't seem to get over whatever grudge they held. It felt like high school all over again.

"Camille, you really need to get over yourself and lose the attitude. It does nothing for your complexion," Reed said.

Camille shot a venomous look at Reed before sauntering toward Jasper.

"I see you've bought your helpless plaything a new store. What's next? This little human will never be part of us,

Jasper. What were you thinking when you mated this piece of trash? She will never be like us. I can't believe you chose her when you could have had me, a real werewolf. Not something that needs to be changed in order to fit in."

Camille's toxic rant disgusted Willow. She knew there were some in the Pack that valued pure lines and magic by birth, but it had never been thrown in her face before.

Jasper growled. "Shut your fucking mouth. You overstep your bounds, Camille. Go back to your little home with your goon and leave my family alone. You are lucky I have honor and don't hit women. But Fredrick, I would run if I were you, I don't have any qualms where you are concerned." His voice was laced with ice.

"I know my place, oh mighty Beta." Camille sneered. "But your human better learn hers." With one last poisonous glare, she stormed out of Willow's new bakery with Fredrick hot on her tail.

"You need to be careful of that one, Jasper. I don't think that is the last we'll be hearing of her." Reed's warning came as no surprise to Willow.

"I know. I know. I have been lax in my Beta responsibilities, I think. It's my job to deal with rumblings of unease." Jasper's voice still held anger, but a bit of sadness as well. What did Camille mean to him? Her pain must have shown on her face because Jasper bent to kiss her lips.

"I never loved her. I don't even like her. She is nothing to me. I'm just sad this is what Camille has become." Jasper shook his head as if to organize his thoughts. "Let's go home. We can celebrate there." He gave a wicked smile, and Willow's pussy clenched. Oh, she wanted to celebrate now.

"On that note, I'm going to Adam's to warn him about the duo of doom. Have fun." With a wave and a smile, Reed left, and they were alone.

"Quickly, I need you." Jasper threw her over his shoulder and ran home. Some days she could really get used to his caveman antics.

By the time they reached their home, Willow panted with need. "What do you do to me?"

"I think the better question is, what am I going to do to you." Jasper's eyes darkened as he growled against her ear, the breath trailing down her neck pulsating against her. "I want you."

"Take me. Please."

Jasper wrapped her hair around his fist and kissed her with bruising force. He unsnapped her jeans and had them down around her ankles before she could blink. She gasped as his fingers twisted the sides of her thong and tore it from her body.

He kissed and nibbled her neck around the fading mate mark before lifting his head and turning her around, bending her over the couch. The rasp of a zipper and rustle of jeans sent shivers over her spine. He danced his fingers across her thighs, before he finally brushed against her clit. She bucked against him, aroused and ready.

"You're wet for me. Do you want me?" He licked her ear and nibbled her lobe.

She moaned and nodded, unable to speak.

Jasper entered her to the hilt in one quick thrust. Stars shattered behind her lids. He barely touched her, and she came. God, she loved this bond. This man. He quickly withdrew before he pistoned into her again and again. The sound of his balls slapping her ass as his thighs rammed hers increased her pulse and desire. With one hand still holding her hair in a firm grip, his other hand crawled up her chest, twisting and pinching her nipples, causing her pussy to tighten around his thick shaft.

He shifted before he plunged into her again, his cock rubbing against her womb. Willow began to ride the crest again, closer and closer to orgasm. His stiffened and released a shout that echoed off the walls as he came, filling her. His seed warmed her. The sound of his release brought her to completion as she cried out his name. After that, their heavy breathing was the only sound in the quiet room.

"I love you, Jasper."

"I love you too." He pulled back and picked her up, before carrying her into their bedroom.

"Where are we going?"

"You didn't think we were done celebrating did you?" Seeing the grin full of promise on his face, she exhaled a happy sigh.

Oh, how she loved celebrating.

THE WOOD beneath his hands felt warm as he carved the banisters for Willow's bakery. He loved working with wood, making this come to life. This was for Willow, his Willow.

"You done fondling that wood?" Reed laughed.

"At least I have something to fondle," Jasper quipped.

"Dude, that's low."

"How is the painting coming?" Reed was painting a mural on one of the walls, and Jasper was in awe of his little brother's talent.

"Almost done. I hope she'll like it."

"I'm sure she will; she loves your work."

"I hope so. She needs something nice, ya know?" Reed smiled.

"Considering she's my mate, I do. I love making her smile."

The door opened and Camille walked in.

Dammit, he hated that woman.

She prowled across the room and ran a well-manicured fingernail down his chest.

"Hello, Jasper," she purred.

"Remove your finger before I remove it for you," he growled.

She stuck out her bottom lip and pouted. But she removed her finger.

"You used to like my touch."

"No, I tolerated it to scratch an itch." He knew he sounded like an ass, but being nice wouldn't get through her thick skull.

"Ouch, Beta has claws." She snarled.

"Camille, what do you want? You don't want me. I sure as hell don't want you."

"I just wanted to see your little mate's new digs. Don't fault me."

He glared at her, not believing her at all.

"I'm the Beta of our Pack. You need to remember the fact that I help lead our people. You do nothing but belittle them." He let out a small glimpse of his power, anger at her pettiness through the past years seeping through. The depth of the strength curling out from his chest to his fingertips, filling the room with its presence, thickening the air.

Her eyes widened, and she buckled under the power, going to her knees in submission.

"Go, Camille. Do not come in here again. Do not bother my mate or my family. Go away. Tell your little goon Fredrick, too. Do you understand me?"

She whimpered and nodded, backing away on her hands and knees, through the door Reed held open.

"Shit, Jasper. Nice show of power. You almost got me to submit." Reed quirked a brow.

Jasper shrugged. "I didn't use it all. I just wanted her out. She's been bothering me for years and being a bitch to everyone. I've been so preoccupied that I haven't been a good Beta. I shouldn't have let her get away with it for so long."

"You know she's not done yet, don't you?" Reed asked.

"I know. Camille will never learn. But she has to know that I won't lie back and take it."

"Good to know."

"Now get back to painting. I want to make this place look amazing for my Willow."

Reed nodded and went back to work.

Jasper smoothed the wood in his palm and got back to what he was good at, what he loved, for the woman he loved.

12

The smell of fresh paint and wood shavings tickled Willow's nose. The tangy scent of male sweat on glistening bodies mixed with the sweet and sugary chocolate aroma from the brownies she'd baked that morning. A luscious and sinful combination if there ever was one.

The marble countertop was cool to the touch as she ran her hand along the smooth edge. The deep, ruby-red velvet inlay of the picture board above the glass panels clung to her fingers. Burgundy and chocolate colored ribbons adorned it, begging for pictures and memories to surface and be known. To be immortalized.

Sounds of hammer pounding nails and a saw slicing into two-by-fours filled her ears, keeping the latent fear at bay. She felt ghostly hands gliding and gripping her arms, forcing her immobile...

No, no, that was over. She was safe. The sounds of metal yielding and arching as the final oven was moved brought her back.

She let out a sigh. *This is mine. Made for me.*

The Jamensons were on the last day of construction for her new bakery in the Den. Everyone had worked together to put in the last sets of shelves and decorations, while Reed focused solely on his mural. Broad brush strokes and minute details covered the large expanse. Dark bold colors of chocolate, cherry and a lighter cream interplayed and entwined to create a masterpiece of lines and shapes. An abstract painting that expressed love and warmth. Beautiful.

Today was also an anniversary of sorts. Four months before, the Central Pack had abducted her from her previous bakery, changing her life forever. Though it frustrated Jasper to no end, her Pack, because they were hers now, had not retaliated against their enemy. During another Pack circle, in which they discussed when and how they would attack, Camille and Fredrick stated that due to the fact Willow was not Pack at the time of her kidnapping, the Redwood Pack could not and should not go after the Centrals. It was against the code and laws of their history and it gave the Centrals a weapon to hurt them. The fury on Jasper's face when they told him caused Willow to shudder. It took every ounce of her strength to stand up to him and say enough was enough. They would not enter the Central's land on a wave of revenge. They'd hold their own.

Though the imprisonment threaded her nightmares, the outcome of her mating with Jasper could not be ignored. Thanks to Hector and Corbin, really. Willow snorted and looked around her new shop.

Tan walls with brown trim that reminded her of chocolate chip cookies were lightened by large windows in the front of her store. Soon, white curtains with brown stripes would accentuate the curve of the windows and pull in the color of the room. Large photos in dark brown, wooden frames hung on the walls. Each picture was of a family member, infusing her bakery with love. Tables and chairs with white and brown tablecloths dotted the floor in front, leaving a walkway to the counter, which would showcase her treats and delicacies.

Her family built this. For her. This was her home. Tears clouded her eyes, but Willow held them back. This was a time for happiness. No crying allowed.

A growl sounded behind her and she turned. Mel sat on the ground with a snarl on her face, and Willow broke out laughing.

"It's not funny." The frustrated look on Melanie's face was priceless. "This stupid curtain rod broke in my hands. I guess I don't know my own strength." With a shrug, she threw the bent pieces of metal away and picked up another.

Melanie's strength and shorter temper had arrived after her first shift two nights prior. Apparently, she'd transformed amazingly well and fit into the life of a werewolf nicely. A sense of jealousy swept through Willow, but she shook it off.

No.

It will happen. Jasper will ask me to change and join the Pack fully.

At least, that's what she told herself.

"What did I say about your stress levels, baby?" Kade's soft growl announced his presence. Mel fell into his open arms with a sigh. "And you really shouldn't be in here with Reed and his paint." His brows furrowed as he brushed a lock of hair from his mate's face.

She suddenly wanted Jasper near her.

Curiosity overcame her and she interrupted the loving couple's moment. "Are the fumes too much for your new senses?"

A slow smile spread over Kade's face.

Okay, she was missing something.

"Kade needs to watch his mouth, but I guess the wolf is out of the bag." Melanie beamed a smile. "We're pregnant."

The shouts of glee and congratulations from the Jamenson family were so loud Willow was sure her new picture frames would vibrate right off the walls.

A baby.

Tears glistened on Pat's face. Edward, in typical Alpha fashion, choked back his emotion. Cailin screeched and threw herself into Kade's arms. Reed gave a laugh and knelt to place a gentle kiss on Mel's still-flat belly, cooing sweet nothings. North pushed their artist brother out of the way.

"Congratulations, my sister wolf." North then proceeded to take her pulse at the wrist, instructing her to 'keep the excitement level to a minimum.' Apparently, he couldn't resist playing doctor even for a moment.

Kade was hugged and roughly slapped on the back as Mel was gently and reverently held and kissed. However, Reed didn't seem to get the "be cautious around the pregnant lady" memo and spun her around the store.

"Get your hands off my woman." Kade's growl only made Reed and Mel laugh harder.

Mel's contagious laughter died slowly as Adam stepped toward her. Willow saw misery flash in his eyes before he blanked his expression, holding Mel in a bone-crushing hug. Pain for her brother-in-law shot through her heart as she remembered that Adam had lost not only his mate but his child.

Jesus. She couldn't even comprehend what he felt right now.

As she shook her head to cast away those saddening thoughts, movement caught her eye. Maddox stood alone in the shadows, the light from the window illuminating his face. Willow sucked in a breath. *His eyes.* Gold radiated and pulsed from his unblinking gaze. Though wolves' eyes glowed during passion and anger, this, she felt, was different. Eerie. She took a step closer, and it hit her. Emotion. A tingling sensation like a thousand fingertips dancing across her skin made her shiver. Maddox was an empath. The empath of the Pack. The feelings of happiness and glee emanating from his family must be overwhelming and spilling from him. With a quirk of his lips, Maddox gave a nod of his head, finally closing his eyes.

Arms wrapped around her from behind, and she sank into Jasper's embrace. Warmth seeped through his touch as Willow watched Kade kiss his mate.

"I want that." Jasper's breath danced along her neck as he spoke closely to her ear. His arm slid down her front, his palm caressing her stomach. Butterflies fluttered within, and she smiled. She'd been wrong before; *this* was home. Four months. Only four months of being his mate, and she already wanted – no, needed – to bear his young.

"Me too." All thoughts of nervousness and trepidation toward the change fled her mind as Jasper bit into the flesh of her earlobe.

"With all of the practicing we've been doing, I think it's only a matter of time. Don't you?"

"Uh huh." Rational thoughts and real words had apparently escaped her.

"Wanna go practice some more?" His deep, throaty laugh vibrated down her spine and she turned in his hold, wrapping her arms around his neck.

"I think that can be arranged." She smiled at him,

watching the love radiate from his eyes. She was at peace in his arms, in her bakery, in their home.

Please, never let this end.

"YOU REALLY MET ON A BLIND DATE?" Willow asked.

"Yep. Odd right?" Melanie laughed.

The two of them sat in Kade and Mel's house, drinking hot chocolate and eating cookies that Willow had baked the night before. The other woman glowed. Pregnancy suited her.

"My friend, Larissa, who's a witch mated into the Pack, set me up with Kade. They all thought we'd get along and have fun. But they had no idea we were mates." Mel explained.

"Fate's tricky like that."

"I didn't believe in fate at the time. I mean, how could I? I'm a chemist. Analytically speaking, fate, mates, and were-wolves shouldn't exist. But here we are." Mel shrugged.

"I take it you didn't react well."

"I was horrible. I left then let Kade fight for me." Mel teared up, and Willow pulled her into a hug. "Sorry, hormones. I should have listened to my heart, but instead I let my brain make all my decisions. I hurt him and myself. I'm just lucky he took me back."

"Mel, of course he took you back. You didn't do anything wrong. You're allowed to take time and think."

Mel let out a breath. "But Kade's going to be Alpha. That means I'm going to be the lead female of this Pack someday. I just don't know if I can gain their respect."

Willow took the other woman's hand. "They already do, Mel. I see the way people come to you for advice. The way they ask you for help with school and other things. Mel, they look up to you. You have their respect. You're going to make a great Alpha female."

Mel sniffed and waved her hand in front of her face. "Thanks, Wil. I hope so. I have the attitude for it, according to Kade." They both laughed. "But enough crying, you came over here for something, right?"

Yep, Mel would be a great Alpha. There was no hiding anything from her.

"I want to change," Willow blurted. "I want to be a wolf. But I don't know how to convince Jasper."

Mel's eyes widened. "I take it Jasper doesn't want that."

"I don't know. He doesn't say anything when I bring it up."

The other woman sighed. "No one can order him to let you. But you do have your own power. If you truly want to, we can make it happen. But you need to find out exactly why he's acting like this. I know Jasper; he's a nice guy and doesn't do anything without a reason."

"I know. I'm just scared."

"Wil, maybe he is too."

Willow sighed. What was she going to do?

13

———

J asper sat in his parents' living room, dread filling his belly. Fear crawled up his back, wrapping its spindly fingers around his throat, choking him. The thoughts and actions he'd tried to repress had caught up with him.

The Centrals wanted Willow back.

Well, that was too damn bad. There was no way they were getting a paw near her. Determination settled on him like a second skin. He took a deep breath, inhaling the familiar scent of his mother's sirloin stew and his father's pipe smoke that was failing miserably at being masked by a wood fire. No doubt his mother would be in the room soon to scold her husband lovingly on his infraction. Jasper smiled at his parents' relationship. It was what he wanted with Willow. What he needed.

Watching Kade go through the turmoil of two circles

and fighting for Tracy, then Melanie, yet rising from the ashes with Melanie by his side, brought feelings of jealousy to Jasper. Before this, Jasper had done his duty. He'd cared for his Pack had been at their beck and call. If a Pack member needed a job, a shoulder to cry on, someone to talk to, Jasper was there. Even calls in the middle of the night used to be the norm. And he'd been okay with it. He laughed with others, helped Reed play practical jokes on their brothers. Yet something had always felt missing. Willow.

And now Hector Reyes and his sadistic bastard of a son, Corbin, were trying to destroy his world and seize his mate.

His wolf growled and clawed to the surface.

"They will not take her. We can protect her. Though, there is a way to make her stronger."

Jasper ignored his wolf, anger spearing his consciousness. Dammit, he couldn't lose her. He couldn't, no wouldn't, let her become a wolf. It was too dangerous. Melanie had been lucky, she survived the change. It wasn't a guarantee. Maybe one in ten wolves actually survived the change. That's why most didn't even try. Fate usually mated wolves to other wolves – not humans. What would he do if Willow died trying to become like him? He loved her the way she was.

He was strong. Dammit, he was the fucking Beta of the Redwood Pack, the third strongest wolf, behind Kade and his father, of the most powerful Pack of the Americas, if not the world. She would be safe with him. He could protect and keep her in his life.

Already, he was making adjustments to their home. Adding touches here and there that excited Willow. It was her place too. He'd bought cooper-bottom pans and other kitchen goodies that made her eyes light up. Together, they'd bought pillows and decorations so their home didn't look so masculine. The need to show her she belonged ran deep. Not only had he built the bakery for her with his own two hands, he was creating a space for the two of them.

His father's voice interrupted his thoughts. "Jasper, are you listening to me?"

"Sorry, Dad." He took another deep breath to calm his nerves, focusing his attention on his Alpha. "What were you saying?"

His father gave him a pointed look before speaking. "Adam's received information that the Centrals demand Willow. They say she was theirs and we didn't have a right to enter their territory and take her. Regardless that she's your mate, they have a point. We did trespass on their territory. But it doesn't matter. She's your mate and they kidnapped her. There are rumors they will cross our border and attempt to take her unless we give her up."

Anger burned in Jasper's veins.

Adam rubbed his jaw before speaking. "Jasper, it gets worse. Corbin is telling others that Willow was his potential mate and he hadn't had the chance to mark her before you showed up. He is saying that you stole her from him without fighting in the circle. He demands reparations."

Jasper shot to his feet in a blind rage. "He thinks to take my mate? My Willow? That barbarous fuck thinks he can speak those vile lies and live?" Blood rushed in his ears, his heart pounding. He clenched his fists, as panic and fear seeped beneath his fury threatening to suffocate him.

"Calm down, son." The Alpha's voice swept over his outrage, soothing his ache. "We know you won't let Corbin take her. He has no claim. We won't allow it." His father's voice was stern and held the power of an ageless force. Pack. Jasper drew in the magic of home, calming himself.

This was what it meant to be Pack. To take in the power surrounding him and bring him home. To calm the wolf and his emotions in order to think rationally. He didn't know how lone wolves did it.

Silent throughout the discussion, Kade rubbed his temples, a sign of frustration and deep thinking. "There is something more. Something darker. Willow was not a potential mate for Corbin. As evil as he is, Corbin could not have allowed her to be hurt as she was if it were true. That means this obviously false statement must be a shroud for their real intentions."

"Magic." Adam's answer brought a flicker of a memory, something that Jasper should know. But what was it?

"They were stuck." At his brothers' and father's obvious confused looks, Jasper continued. "The wolves at the

Central's compound where we found Willow. Adam, don't you remember what Reed said? They were stuck. They didn't follow us, as if a magical barrier held them in place. It was magic; I'm sure of it."

"But what type of magic could do this?" Adam asked. "What are the Centrals hiding?"

"Could they be working with the witches?" Kade asked.

Jasper shook his head. "I don't think so. The magic felt different. Oily. Almost sliding against my skin. I almost forgot that. I was too worried for Willow and getting us out of there at that point."

"I've never heard of magic like that." His dad added. "But I am relatively young. We may need to ask the elders." Again his father's voice calmed his worries. It felt good to be with family.

"Magic should not taste tainted," Adam said with a deep growl. "Witches are in tune with the Earth, and are part of it. Witch magic should feel earthy like freshly dug soil, floral like just bloomed flowers, fresh like the wind brushing your face, warm like the sun dancing across your skin, or cool like sliding your hands across clean and clear water. That is magic. Not slick and oily."

Sometimes his brother surprised him with how much he knew about others' culture, though as the Enforcer of the Pack, it was his job not only to protect them from the outside world but to understand the outside world as well.

"Witch magic is hereditary," Adam continued. "In most

cases they heal or do good. There are few that are truly powerful."

"The magic that is inherent in the Pack is different as well," his father interrupted. "It provides proof of strength and family." Jasper nodded, urging his father to continue the story he knew well, told to him as a young pup.

"Though it is legend, it is said that werewolves were formed from the Moon Goddess. Saddened by the atrocities of man and the weakening of their souls, the Moon Goddess stepped down from her ivory crescent throne and walked among the dense forests and rivers.

"There she found a hunter deep in the brush, searching for his next kill. The Goddess knew this man must eat and provide for his family, but she was disheartened at the depravity of the souls she watched over. The act of free will was not unknown to her, so she stood back and waited for the decisions the hunter made.

"A rustling of leaves alerted them both to an approaching beast. The hunter took aim with his bow and struck a gray wolf, injuring it but not killing the animal. He walked over to his prey, leaning over it, as the Moon Goddess drew nearer to the two, thoughts of redemption wafting through her.

"Startled by the Goddess presence, the hunter bowed yet stood protective over his kill. The Goddess told him that man needed to understand the connection between Earth and man. The man, confused, was unprepared for the magic pulsating and shocking through his system when the Goddess bent and touched her palm to his heart and the wolf's.

"That night, she created the first werewolf. Not man, nor beast, but a blending of the two. Man would dominate and walk the world, yet the wolf would remain internal forever, always challenging man's wants and desires. During times of the full moon, the Moon Goddess's pull is immense, non-tactile entity and man will change into the beast he hunted and killed, running through the forest of Earth on four paws rather than two feet. In times of great stress and need, man can choose to be wolf.

"The magic that the Moon Goddess placed on us that night in the forest still runs through our veins. It is earthy and good. Though we are human, we do carry within us a savage and uncivilized element that drives us. Our magic connects us, and it is not evil." Jasper's Alpha closed his eyes, bowing his head.

"If the Centrals are using magic, it's not from a wolf. It is their human selves that harbor evil, not their inner magic," Kade said. As the Heir of the Pack, he most understood his wolf.

"So you're telling me what we felt was not from witches, and we know it was not werewolf magic. So what was it?" Jasper's question silenced the room.

What had the Centrals unleashed?

Jasper's muscles clenched at the thought. After

reviewing everything they knew, it seemed their enemies were touching something unknown and dangerous. Even though it may only be a ploy, they still wanted his mate. His Willow.

"I won't let them take her, no matter what evil they uncover." Jasper's growl was low, seething. He was edgy, the skin rippling on his forearms. His need to hunt was urgent, yet he wouldn't leave Wil alone, unprotected. His palms itched as the necessity to build something, to create with his hands took hold. If he couldn't kill his enemies now, he would expunge his energy somehow.

"Of course, Jasper. Willow is safe with us." Kade stood and walked over then kneeled before him. "I vow to protect your mate with all I have in me." The magic of his words snapped in place within Jasper. For Kade to vow this, while his own mate was pregnant, touched him deeply.

A binding vow and agreement through their wolves. They'd go to the grave to protect Willow and fight by his side.

"I, too, vow." Adam took Kade's place, and again, the magic washed over him.

"I vow, son, to protect your mate, my daughter."

"Dad, what if this is a ruse? What then? What do they want from us?" Jasper asked, needed to ask the obvious question.

Edward sighed. "I don't know. Maybe power? They're

the second ranked Pack in the Americas below us. It's the only thing I can think of."

"Then we need to stop them. No matter what." Jasper growled.

If only it were that easy.

14

"Honestly, Wil, the smells emanating from this basket are killing me. Can't we stop and eat before we go to the circle?" Jasper's plea and boyish grin not only made Willow laugh but surprised her.

For the past few days, Jasper's demeanor bordered on distant, if not cold. At first, she'd thought it was something she'd done, but his attitude wasn't unique. The entire Jamenson family was on edge. Tension floated on the air, thickening as time passed. Something was coming. Willow didn't know what, but she kept on alert.

"If you want to explain to a group of hungry wolves where their food went, go for it. But I'm not Little Red Riding Hood on the way to grandmother's house. I will not ask 'What big teeth you have' and give you my food."

Standing next to her, Jasper kissed the top of her head and held her close. "You know it's not food I want, my Willow," he murmured in her ear, sending goose bumps down her arms.

"You know we don't have time for that."

"That's not what you said this morning when you took me in hand to teach me a lesson about laundry." He quirked a brow, and Willow blushed. *Damn him.*

"It isn't my fault that you refuse to sort your laundry. For a wolf who is over a hundred years old, I'd think you'd actually know how to do it yourself."

Jasper tickled her side, and she almost lost her basket.

"Hey, watch the food, baby. You do realize that if you'd just let me hold the damn thing, we wouldn't have this problem." At her defiant look he continued, "And I do know how to sort laundry. I just don't sort it into twelve different piles. Lights and darks work well for me."

Willow loved this playful side of him. She'd missed it this past week.

"Are we really going to start this conversation again? I mean really, it's laundry. And if I remember clearly, you got your way. I sort, you do the folding." Her teeth bit into her lip as she thought back to exactly how they came to that arrangement.

The smug look on his face indicated his thoughts were on the same path. *Men.*

"What can I say? This whole domestic bliss thing kinda fits."

"That's what you say now, but once I start having you do dishes, you're gonna run in fear."

"I don't run in fear from anyone. And I've been doing my own dishes since before you were born. Just –" Jasper's stopped and flared his nostrils.

Willow stopped behind him, her gaze on the woods surrounding them.

"Jasper, what–"

He held his finger to his lips and she shut up. *What's going on?*

"Willow, I want you to run back to the house and lock the doors," he said, his voice low, angry, and laced with fear.

"Jasper, no. I'm not going to leave you." Fear may have a hold on her, but she wouldn't leave his side for anything. Not while he was alone.

He cursed under his breath, and glared. Gone was his joyful expression from earlier. The cold brutality of his Beta power settled in over his face like a stern mask.

"Now." His voice low, threaded with anxiety.

"Jasper, I can help."

"I can't focus on you and whatever is out there. I need you to go. Now."

Fear crept up her spine; danger lurked around the corner. She rose to her tip-toes and brushed his lips in a gentle kiss.

"Be safe." *Please, I can't lose you.*

"Run, Willow. I love you."

"I love you, too."

The basket fell from her hands, the contents spilling to the ground, as Willow ran toward their home. Her chest burned from exhaustion as she climbed the hill. A howl split into the night, causing her to panic.

How far had they walked?

The hair on her arm prickled her skin and she stopped. Something was out there. In front of her, blocking her path? Or behind her?

Damn it, she didn't want to be the dumb chick in the horror movie who ran into a trap. Why had she left Jasper?

Something tugged on her brain, and she looked toward where the path led to the forest. Why did she want to go in there? She bit her lip and took a step closer to the darkness. Another howl echoed in the air, and she took another step. She needed to see what was past the line of trees. Some sort of magnetism drew her in, clouding her thoughts. Every time she tried to back away she only moved farther in.

Fear crawled up her spine, but she kept moving.

Great, now she really *was* the dumb chick who dies first in the horror movie.

Despite her uneasiness, Willow moved into dense forest, leaves rustling against her cheek and sides, as she walked. The large trees rose up toward the sky, reaching for the light, as worshipers would their god. The canopy stopped the light almost fully in some places, making it hard to see. Damn it, she really missed Jasper.

Dead leaves crunched under her feet as she ventured farther. The thick trees muted the outside noises, creating a tomb like feeling. A large lump on the forest floor stood out against the fading light. Willow squinted her eyes, praying they would adjust to the darkness. In times like these, she wished she were a werewolf. The disparity on the ground didn't move as she walked toward it, holding her breath.

A twig dug into her knee as she knelt down beside it. Finally, her eyes adjusted so she could get a good look. And screamed.

THE SOIL SIFTED between his paws as Jasper sniffed the ground. He shouldn't have sent Willow off. Why had he done that? He shook his head, trying to clear out the cloudiness. Something dug into his brain, not letting him think.

When he'd first inhaled that tangy scent with Willow, he needed to get distance from her. Like in a trance, he yelled at her to leave him and not stay by his side where he could protect her. No, he had told her to run away alone, with no help. A command that he in his normal thinking self, he would never have made. Something urged him to let her go off on her own with a threat around them and run the opposite direction. When she ran, he'd shifted, bones rearranging, muscles tearing, and after that Jasper had followed the tangy scent into the forest, away from his mate. He howled at the power suppressing his mind

"*Magic.*"

Finally. His wolf hadn't spoken to him since he'd begun his walk with Willow. Someone had laid a magical trap for him and her, and they'd walked right into it. Damn it. He howled again, a pain=filled howl. Why the hell would someone try to trap them?

As a wolf, his senses were sharper, more attuned to the Earth. Though before he'd felt the need to be in this part of the territory, he knew now that nothing would be found here. He'd been duped, and so had his wolf. By magic.

A scream pierced the silence. *Willow.*

On four paws, he ran through the overgrowth of the natural forest, not caring that branches tugged at his fur. His mate's scream sent dread through him. Once he found her, oh and he would, he would kill the sick fuck that separated them.

Maddox might be the one who would kill quickly and effectively to avoid feeling the pain and fear. But, like Adam, Jasper would torture. Before he gutted them, they would suffer.

His heart thudded in his ears as he followed their matebond to his Willow. Thank God they'd completed the connections so he could always find her, barring outside forces.

Willow screamed again just as he jumped over a rotted log. She stood over a lifeless body, her face pale in shock. Her brown hair fell lank in her face, over her wide, frightened eyes. When she caught sight of his wolf, she visibly exhaled in relief. Jasper lowered his head and pulled his magic to turn back into a man. Though it hurt slightly, his age dampened the pain of transformation.

Naked, he knelt and took Willow into his arms. Her body felt cool against his overheated, sweat-slick chest.

"Shh, Wil, it's okay. I'm here." But he almost hadn't been. Some outside force had pulled at them, edging them apart, trying to put chinks in their armor.

"Jasper." A soft whisper. "Why did I leave? Why did I come here?"

"I don't know exactly. But we'll find out." And those responsible would pay.

With Willow still in his arms, her breath still raspy against his chest, he finally looked down at the corpse at their feet.

A woman's body lay perfectly on the floor, her hands clasped on her chest reminiscent of Snow White in the fairy tale. If it hadn't been for the bruising, cuts, and blood, she would almost look peaceful. Light brown hair surrounded a pale, gray face with glassy, hazel eyes. Willow's eyes.

Cold dread gripped its icy fingers around his heart as

the implications of the body sank in. A message. And not very subtle.

"Jasper, she looks like me."

"Come on baby, let's get out of here." He stood up, unmindful of his nudity, and tried to walk Willow away from the sight he thought would haunt her nightmares. He knew they would haunt his.

"Wait." She grabbed his hand in a surprisingly firm grip. "There's a note."

Jasper pushed her behind him. She'd seen enough already tonight. He knelt toward the body, trying not to look at the face that so closely resembled his love that his heart hurt, and carefully took the note from her hands.

Keep yours close.

Three words. Three simple words and Jasper's wolf clawed to the surface to protect their Willow. Fire ran through his veins, and he had the courage to do what he should have done in the beginning. He bent over the woman and inhaled her scent. A soft floral over crushed stone. Talon Pack. They resided on the other side of the Central Pack in Montana and were their allies and friends. The Talons were low in the power rankings of the Packs but protective of their own. How they hell had the Centrals taken her and brought her here?

Fuck.

"Let's go home. I need to call my father and brothers."

A nod.

Damn it. He knew it wasn't over. The family had just talked about it. Vows were spoken. Yet, somewhere deep down, he'd prayed it wouldn't come to this.

War.

15

Back at the house, Jasper paced in their living room. The Centrals had a lot of nerve. Coming onto his land and bringing a fucking witch with them. Not that he had a prejudice against witches. Far from it. He trusted them with his Pack's protection, healing, and in some cases, friendship. But the fact that they would align themselves with their rivals and use tainted magic left a bitter taste on his tongue.

"That reminds me, that tangy smell from the forest. Why was it different?"

Jasper cocked his head at his wolf's question. Yes, not a pure witch's scent. But what? Unlike in some folk-lore, there was no such thing as black or white magic. A witch's magic came from their soul and the earth and smelled of earthly things. The sickly sweet smell shadowing the forest just an hour ago was not of earth. Hector and Corbin were meddling with something deeper than normal magic.

The dark entity from the night of his marking Willow came to mind. Who was he? His instincts told him that whoever the ally the Centrals had found, it was not of this world. Something new. Tainted. Something to fear.

Jasper took a deep, ragged breath. Whatever deals their enemies had made, not all were revealed. An unknown magical entity aided the Centrals, bent on taking his mate, though Jasper had a feeling that wasn't their prime objective. No, they wanted something else. Desiring Willow was just a cover, a distraction. And a damn good one.

"Jasper."

He stopped pacing and looked at Willow. Her pulse beat rapidly, moving against the slick sheen of sweat on her neck. Eyes bright, she blinked, yet her fear remained. Tonight was not the first time she'd seen a dead body. No, her parents' held that honor. The accident that claimed their lives had also ripped her innocence away. The wet road and the inebriated driver combined in an interplay of dilapidated metal and glass had forced his Willow into foster homes and away from their comfort.

Now, because of Jasper's mark and his *forced* mark, she'd lost some of the inherent innocence of being human.

"Do not blame yourself, Jasper. The blame belongs solely on the Centrals' shoulders. Willow is yours. Ours."

Jasper desperately wanted to believe his wolf so he

could take Willow in his arms and tell her he loved her. Tell her everything would be okay. But he couldn't. Words escaped him.

"Jasper."

The confusion in her voice brought him out of his thoughts.

"Yes, Willow?" God, how he loved her. He would do anything to protect her. Even from the things she didn't know could hurt her.

"When we were out there, something took me from you. I didn't want to leave, to run. But I did. Why?"

"Whatever killed that girl had a form of magic I've never seen. You didn't run away they took you." That thought scared the shit out of him.

"I felt so helpless out there. I don't want to feel that way anymore."

Her gaze rested on him, pleading for his help. His heart broke for her. No, he didn't want that either.

"I need to change, Jasper. I need to become one of you. It's the only way."

Logically, he knew she was right. However, the prideful male in him resented the inclination. He clenched his fists as his wolf clawed to the surface. Anger for those who stole her safety made him see red.

"Jasper. Watch your words."

He ignored his wolf. "It's too dangerous. You saw what my father did to Melanie. He almost killed her. I don't want you to go through that. The pain of the change is excruciating. And even after the biting and tearing of your flesh, there is no guarantee you will even be a wolf. You could die. I won't risk that."

"But isn't it worth a try?"

"And once you do," He couldn't listen to her words. If he did, she could be hurt. There was nothing more important to him than her health and safety. He continued as if she hadn't spoken "And once you do, you'd have to deal with the fact that you've lost your humanity. You'd be a wolf. An animal."

"Don't say that. I don't think of you as one. I love you."

He gave a joyless laugh at her declaration.

"I may walk on two legs, but I have urges just like any animal. I could kill you at a moment's notice if I didn't control myself. I don't want you to deal with that."

"That wouldn't be an issue if I was a wolf just like you. I could hold my own."

"But then you would be forced to control your strength with others. To deal with that inner pain."

"So you would rather me die of old age, while you remain young?"

"I would rather have you safe but for a few decades then dead at my father's hand."

Her mouth gaped open and her eyes welled. But her tears didn't fall.

What the fuck was he doing? Why was he picking a fight

with her? Yes, these thoughts were not new. But he could've spoken rationally with her. Now he was cutting her down because some sick fuck had scared him with the images of losing her.

"*Fix this. You hurt her.*"

His wolf, again, spoke true.

"I can't believe you just said that." Willow's voice held a trace of pain, but that slight pain was overshadowed by her anger.

He opened his mouth to speak, but she held up her hand.

"All this time I thought you would change your mind. I sat back patiently waiting for you to realize that, if I didn't change, I would die. Leaving you alone. Reed told me to wait, that you would come around. And I stupidly believed him."

She'd spoken to her brother about this? His thoughts jumbled as he panted in anger.

Willow heaved a breath and continued, "I don't understand you, Jasper. You say you love me, yet you don't want to be with me forever? If you love me so much, why can't you give me the tools for me to protect myself?"

"Are you saying I'm not strong enough to protect you?"

"Oh, you stupid wolf! That's not what I'm saying at all. And you know it."

Damn it, he didn't want to fight with her. What the fuck? The Centrals didn't want his Willow. No, they wanted to hurt his Pack. This whole mess lay on his shoulders. If he hadn't been so brazen as to take a human mate and hadn't failed to protect her in the first place, this never would have happened.

"I never should have walked into that bakery," he whispered. "I never should have chosen you. This shouldn't have happened."

He knew he whispered his pain at his failures at protecting his mate, yet he didn't know Willow had heard until he looked up and saw her face.

Pain. Utter betrayal. Hurt crossed her face as the first tear fell down her pale cheek.

"Dammit, Jasper. She doesn't know what you mean."

"Willow, that's not–"

Again, she held up a hand and shook her head.

"I see." No emotion. No more tears.

The love of his life simply blinked twice then walked out the door. Out of his life.

THE DOOR CLOSED QUIETLY BEHIND her as Willow walked to the end of the patio. A cool breeze chilled her bare arms, yet she couldn't feel it.

I never should have walked into that bakery. I never should have chosen you. This shouldn't have happened.

Throat too dry to swallow, she shook head, begging for

rational thoughts. Those words. How could he have said that? Daunting pain cascaded through her body as a chasm opened in her heart. A fog settled over her as she slowly stepped off the porch to the path leading away from their home. No, his home. Confusion and loss swallowed her whole in a pain that fractured her heart, pulsating down her arm, tingling her fingers. It was like when a limb fell asleep, but she couldn't move for fear, if she did, she'd lose feeling forever.

Jasper didn't want her.

Willow walked to a bench at the end of the path and sat down slowly. What would she do now? All her life she'd been alone, struggling to find connections. Had she tried too hard? Made something out of nothing? Jasper had come into her bakery and asked her out on a single date. He didn't ask to have her shackled to him. He didn't even want her around long enough to be his true mate. He would wait for her to die off then find a mate he actually wanted. Her mark was simply a pity bite so she didn't have to die in the hands of Corbin and his cronies.

How was she going to get home? Did she even have a home? How was she going to live without him? A chill of loneliness spread over her. She couldn't breathe. Everything was gone. Destroyed. Sobs locked in her throat, but her tears wouldn't fall.

Willow sprang from the bench and blindly ran into the forest. Away from the pain and loss that Jasper brought with him. It wasn't smart or safe, but who cared? She just needed a minute to breathe. Then she'd leave and move on. She wouldn't wallow. That wouldn't solve anything. After a few minutes she stopped, her breath coming in ragged pants.

A branch cracked, shattering the illusion of safety and silence around her. Willow went on alert. Dammit, why had she just left leave like that? She looked over her shoulder as a shadow passed. She opened her mouth to scream, but a hand came behind her and closed over her mouth.

She felt a painful prick in her arm, and as her mind became fuzzy, she realized the prick had been a needle injecting something into her bloodstream. She fought to keep her eyes open, praying she would see her attacker.

"Shh, Willow. You'll be taken care of."

That voice. She knew that voice, yet she couldn't pull her thoughts together. The person behind her lifted her up and carried her deeper in to the forest. She tried to scream again as she struggled against the oncoming blackness but could find no energy to make a sound.

Jasper wouldn't come for her this time.

Willow opened her eyes and, for the second time in her life, woke in a strange room. She blinked, her eyes straining against the bright overhead lights. Memories of a voice and a needle flooded her mind. Not again.

Unlike her last kidnapping – *geez that sounds pathetic* – she wasn't locked away, chained in a dungeon. No, this time she lay across a magnificent king-sized bed, sinking into the lush mattress and surrounded by down pillows and comforters. All in all, quite a different arrangement.

Dark colors filled the room. A deep royal blue antique finish layered the walls with a textured design that soothed yet made her feel closed in. Heavy, gray drapes covered the large windows blocking all natural light, but the overhead light illuminated the room in an eerie glow. Cherry furniture carved with plump cherubs stood in place around her. The gaze from the cherubs' little eyes bore down on her, their presence sucking in the stale air, suffocating her.

Crap, why was she lying there, thinking about the decorations in the room and creepy accessories? Apparently, being taken hostage numerous times had taken a toll on her brain. She needed to get out of here. She tried to swallow, but the cotton taste in her mouth caused her tongue to stick to the roof of her mouth.

"Water?"

At the sound of the voice so near her. Willow screamed.

"Oh no, precious, you mustn't do that."

The cruel man who'd held her chains the last time, Corbin, smiled. He walked to the side of the bed with a glass of water in his hand, the coolness of the glass condensing the water droplets in the stifling humidity of the room. He set the glass on the table and sat on the bed next to her. She wanted to scream again, but she wouldn't. Because he could kill her at any moment, she didn't need to antagonize him.

"Here, my darling, drink up. We can't have you dying of thirst, can we?" He smirked and she cringed.

She didn't want to *die* at all. And why the hell was he acting so nice? This sickly pleasant Corbin worried her more than the yelling man she'd met before. Though her hands were free, his reflexes were far faster than hers even when she was at her best. No, attacking him here without a plan would not be wise. Dammit, she wished Jasper were here.

Great. Why did she have to think about him? He didn't even want her anymore. How pathetic could she get?

He placed the glass to her closed lips. What if he drugged her?

"I've already drugged you. I'm not in the mood to do more at the moment. Drink." His voice carried a lethal edge, sending shivers down her spine.

She opened her mouth, letting the cool liquid slide down her achy throat. She gulped as he tipped the glass more, forcing her to finish it all. Fear pooled in her stomach. No matter her thoughts, Corbin held the control, the power. Even a simple task such as drinking would be on his terms. Not hers. Willow forced herself not to cry. Even a single tear would allow the monster a victory over her that she couldn't allow. She only prayed that his mood wouldn't change until she found a way out. Bile rose in her throat at what he could do when she lost consciousness, or what would happen if she didn't.

Oh God, I just want to go home.

A sob choked her as she remembered she had no home.

"Oh don't cry, my pet." Corbin took a cloth napkin and dabbed the corner of her mouth and eyes. "Nothing good comes of crying. And I haven't done anything to warrant your begging for redemption yet."

She bit her lip and forced herself not to cry out.

Corbin slowly slid his hand down her neck, across the bite Jasper had left the night before, then down her arm, to rest on her stomach. That's when she realized sometime during her captivity, they'd changed her into a soft cotton, low-cut blue dress. She shuddered at the thought of Corbin's hands on her bare skin. He bunched the fabric in his fist and leaned over her.

His nostrils flared as he spat, "You smell like that bastard. I'm going to have great joy in replacing that." He smiled again, and she closed her eyes, afraid of his wrath.

The feel of his fingers on her knee as he brushed her skin made her stomach revolt. *Oh God, I don't want him to touch me.* Memories of her last time with him and the feel of his hands assailed her. In those few short months with Jasper, she hadn't forgotten Corbin liked playing with her. Those instances of vulnerability and the inability to protect herself still haunted her. She didn't want any new horrors added to her already shaky past.

"You never should've left. You can't imagine all the pain that went into getting you here again. Well, I suppose you will know the pain soon enough, won't you?" Corbin tilted his head and laughed. Her stomach almost heaved to spew the remnants of her lunch.

Willow took a deep breath and thought on what he said. How had he accomplished entering Redwood land to take her? Had he had help? The familiar voice before the needle prick came to mind. Who'd attacked her? She tried to think, but something fogged her mind. Dammit, it was right there but faded out of her reach. Could it have been magic? She didn't know enough about witches and other paranormals to really make a guess. Ignorance of the unknown grated on her.

"Honestly, Willow. You need to pay attention." Corbin gripped her chin, forcing her gaze to his. "That's better, my sweet. Now, why did you leave me? We were just getting to the fun part when that bastard pup took you from me. You were a naughty girl, letting him bite you like that in front of my Pack and his brothers. *Tsk tsk.* I think I could do something with that vixen you hide." He leaned over and brushed his lips against hers. Tears leaked from her eyes as she tried not to pull away, afraid he'd do worse than kiss her if she did.

Corbin licked her tears and moaned. "Fearful tears. One of my favorites. Now that Jasper tossed you to the curb, I can take you. At least until I get tired of you. But if you're a good girl, that can be a long, long while."

How did he know that? Jasper, please come for me.

Dammit, she couldn't just sit here and take this. As quickly as she could, she clawed her hand against his face and scratched him with her nails. *Thank God for her new manicure, courtesy of Cailin.* While he howled in surprise, she kneed him in the groin and jumped off the bed, the door in sight.

Hands wrapped around her waist and threw her in to the

wall. Stars and swirls shattered behind her eyelids as the side of her head slammed into the wall. Corbin's fingers dug into her arm, pain ricocheting from his firm grip. He pulled her to his chest, inhaling her scent, before throwing her down to the bed.

Willow screamed, frantically trying to run for her life through her dazed mindset. Her attacker slapped her hard across the face, splitting her lip. He took her arms and legs, chaining them to the bed with a built-in harness. His ease at the task almost made her vomit.

"I told you not to fight. I'm going to enjoy teaching you how to obey." His voice revolted her and caused a nasty shiver to slide down her body.

"Corbin!" Hector's voice bellowed in the room. "Get off her. You can play later. We have things to discuss first."

Willow sighed in relief when Corbin stood and walked to stand behind Hector as the other man walked into the room. She tensed again when she looked up and saw she was now in a room with two men who could rip her to shreds in a second and a third who felt familiar.

The man had dark hair and dark eyes, and he tilted his head and stared at her. If he hadn't looked like he could kill her and enjoy doing it, she thought he could pass for a wicked angel. But there was nothing angelic about the man when he smiled at her.

Oh God, he's worse than Corbin. Darker.

When she took a deep breath to gather her courage for

what was to come, she detected a hint of sulfur on the air. What the hell had the Centrals done?

"Willow, child. I'm glad you could be with us today." Hector smiled at her, and she scoffed? Really?

She must have spoken out loud because his smile slipped just a bit. Though he didn't resonate a true evil quality, as Corbin and the other man did, Hector still carried a ruthless power that curled out from his pores.

He sat on the bed, taking the seat Corbin had vacated. He leaned over her and brushed the hair from her face.

"What do you want?" Her voice sounded rusty, pained.

Hector smiled a sad smile and whispered, "Darling, you're just a tool. A necessity. Something to be used and discarded when the time comes."

She needed Jasper. No matter what happened between the two of them, she still loved him. He would come. He had to.

"You should've just stayed with us," Hector said. "But now we have to deal with you. It's no offense to you, darling. But business is business. Power is power." His eyes glowed when he said it. His wolf must be rising to the surface. She prayed he held control.

"Why are you doing this?" Tears ran down her cheeks, pooling on the sides of her face and into the pillow.

Hector sighed as if he regretted even talking to her. But if she kept talking, that would give her more time to plan her escape. If she could. Plus any information he gave could prove useful. At least she hoped.

"The Redwoods have too much power." His chest heaved as he passionately spewed his diatribe. "They think they are superior, but they are nothing. Weak. Pathetic. It should be me. My Pack. Those fucking Redwoods took too much from me. Bastards."

"The fucking arrogant assholes blend into the humans, thinking them equals. That is a disgrace to who we are, what we can do. We are werewolves; yet they don't relish their strength. No, they just dictate what the other Packs can do. Well, that will be no more. Soon, the Redwoods will understand exactly who they are messing with and who will be their master."

All three men laughed. They were crazy. Utterly insane. And they held her captive.

"Nobody understands my brilliance except my son. But they will."

This couldn't be going anywhere good.

"You see, my wife thought she'd go against me. She took our daughters and tried to run to those Redwoods. She underestimated me, but don't worry, I took care of her. And just to make sure she knew her last act wouldn't go punished with merely her death, I made sure she knew one of her daughters would die for the greater good."

Holy shit. He'd killed his own wife and daughter for his psychotic plan? She needed to get the hell out of here.

"Corbin is strong and will walk beside me as we kill the other Packs. All of them. He will help me rule."

Willow looked over at the crazy man's son and saw an odd smile on his face. He was hiding something, but she had no clue what, but something other than the craziness was going on in this family. Maybe she could use it. She inwardly sighed. Yeah, right. What could she do? She was alone. No Jasper. Any self-defense moves he'd taught her wouldn't work against werewolves. Why hadn't she changed already? Resentment and anger over Jasper's betrayal rose up again, but she stamped it down. This was not the time to reminisce over a lost love.

"And because of the generous sacrifice of my daughter, I now have my ally, Caym." He turned and swept his arm out, bringing their attention to the dark angel in the room.

"Caym is a demon, bound to me and my purpose. I may have had to kill my niece and daughter to accomplish this, but it's no matter. I have another daughter if needed. And with the aid of Caym, and the other demons he will bring forth, we can kill the Redwoods and rule. And once I am the Master Alpha of all the Packs, I will kill the humans or use them as slave labor, finally bringing them down to their rightful place."

The depth and depravity of his plans sickened her. If not for her own survival, she needed to get out and tell someone what she'd been told.

"Why are you telling me this?" She knew her voice couldn't hide her fear, as she choked out the words.

Hector smirked at her and patted her bound hand.

"Because, dear, you will die soon."

That's what she thought he'd say. She wasn't ready to die. Not by a long shot. Her heart sped and she clenched her fists.

"I will slowly and painfully beat you until I am satisfied. Then I will give you to Corbin, who will peel the skin from your body. Finally, we will leave you for dead. There will be no escape, he will not be able to save you and you can't stop us. Who, my dear, could you tell then?"

Willow finally lost her battle with her nerves, screamed.

17

————

The door closed hard with a click, and Jasper stood on the other side, numb. She'd left. Fuck. That wasn't what he'd meant to say. He only meant to prove to her that it was his fault, not hers. That the Centrals wanted her because he chose her. Not because he didn't want her. That was the furthest thing from the truth. He loved Willow more than breath, yet when the words tumbled from his lips, he hadn't thought of the ramifications. Holy hell. What had he done?

Unable to deal with the feelings that overwhelmed him, Jasper sat and stared into space, thinking of all that had gone wrong and all the ways he'd failed her. Finally, after what seemed like hours, he felt the nudge of his wolf, so strong it was almost impossible to ignore.

"You broke our mate's heart, then let her walk out of this

house. Go out there and fix it, or you aren't the Beta I thought you were."

His wolf's disappointed tone cut deep. Shit, he needed to get to her.

Jasper shifted his feet to the door and opened it, praying she'd merely walked to the patio to compose herself and might be sitting there still. When he found it empty, Jasper's heart sank just a little bit more. He inhaled, finding that sweet cinnamon scent, and followed it down the path. He trailed it until he came upon a bench. The scent was concentrated in that spot, as if she'd sat there for a while. Curious and getting more worried, Jasper again walked along the path until he found her scent once more, this time hovering near the entrance to the forest.

What the hell had she been thinking walking into the dense brush right after they'd found that body?

"She wasn't thinking, dumbass. You destroyed her."

His heart raced as he agreed with this wolf. He quickly jogged into the forest, hoping she would be there. *Please God, let her be there.* Finally, after what felt like too long a trek, he found a flattened part of the undergrowth where she must have sat down. But where had she gone?

A shift in the breeze and another murky wolf's scent carried on the wind. Along with that was a tangy sweet scent. Fuck. The scents weren't strong, rather a muted replica of their former selves. They surrounded the place where Willow rested, yet no trail left the spot, as if some-thing magical had swept it away.

Oh God.

They'd taken her.

Again.

Jasper fell to his knees, pain ricocheting from his heart down his body. He howled in agony. Bile rose to his throat as he fought the urge to vomit.

He'd failed. Again. Tears streaked his face as anger burned through his veins. Those fuckers would pay.

His wolf howled, slamming into Jasper's body, begging for release. Claws erupted from his fingertips, as he fought for control. He couldn't shift. Not now. He needed to be human to find her. To get help. His muscles and tendons stretched along his back as his bones began to break. Jasper inhaled, struggling for control.

"Not now." His voice sounded guttural. Fuck, his facial bones were already reconstructing themselves.

He closed his eyes and pulled on the power within. The urge to change subsided, as the power washed over his body, soothing his wolf.

Thank God.

He reached into his pocket and pulled out his phone. His fingers shook as he dialed Adam's number. As the enforcer, Adam would know what to do, rather than run in half-cocked without a plan. Jasper's mind was too muddled and pained to formulate one.

The phone rang twice before Adam finally answered.

"Hello?" Adam's voice sounded slurred from sleep.

"Adam, they took her. Come to the forest outside our home." His voice broke at the end, pain and hurt again radiating throughout his body.

Adam growled. "Fuck. I'm on my way. Don't move" The connection ended with a click, and Jasper put away his phone.

He sat on the spot where Willow had lain, tears dropping onto the dead leaves. They needed to find her, save her before the Centrals did to her what they did to that Talon wolf.

What would he do when he found her? Not if, but when. How could she ever forgive him for letting her be kidnapped? What could he do?

"Jasper." Adam's voice startled him.

Shit, he needed to get his mind off the unknown and find Willow.

"What happened?"

"We fought, and she left."

Adam's eyes darkened. "I see. Fought about what?"

"She wants to go through the transformation. But I said it was too risky. I couldn't lose her."

His brother's voice deepened. "Go on."

Jasper gulped. "Then I said I shouldn't have gone into her bakery. Because I did, she was in danger. I know I'm an idiot. I didn't mean it the way it sounded."

Adam's fist connected with his jaw, almost breaking the bone. Caught off guard, he couldn't keep his balance and he flung backwards, his head slamming into the ground.

"What the fuck?" Jasper snarled.

"Let me get this straight. You told your mate she wasn't good enough to be a wolf."

Jasper opened his mouth to defend himself, but Adam leaned down and punched him again.

"I'm not done yet. After you said it was okay that she'd die long before you did, you then told her you never should have been with her in the first place. Did I miss anything?" Adam's chest rose and fell in heavy pants.

"That is not exactly how it happened, nor was it my intent." But coming from Adam's lips, he was surprised Willow hadn't stabbed him before walking out the door. He sounded like an ass. A cruel and uncaring ass.

"You won't be hearing any argument from me."

"Fuck your intent. Don't you know how lucky you are? You have a mate. And you let her walk out of the house after you practically ripped her heart out. I would kill you myself if it wouldn't upset Mom."

"I know what I said doesn't make sense. But don't you see? It was my fault she got hurt in the first place."

"You egotistical bastard. No, it wasn't. That fucking lunatic Hector and his equally crazy son, Corbin, are the ones at fault for putting her in danger. Not you."

"Fine. But if I let her change—"

"Let her? You fucking idiot. You don't *let* your mate do anything. She's her own person. If she wants to change into a wolf, and it sounds like she does, she probably only wanted your approval because she loves you and wants to make you happy."

Dammit. His heart hurt. Why was he such an idiot?

"But the shift is dangerous. I couldn't risk losing her." The last of his arguments sounded lame and unworthy even to his own ears.

"So you would let her die?"

"I didn't want her to be killed from the change."

"But you would rather lose your mate than have her by your side into your years?"

"Adam, you above all, know what it's like to lose a mate. I didn't want to lose her." As soon as the words left his lips, he wanted to take them back.

His younger brother slammed into his body, forcing him back to the ground. Adam straddled his body, fists flying. Jasper put his arms in front of his face to protect himself, but didn't hit back. He deserved it.

Adam hit and clawed, screaming in agony. Jasper had always known there was pain and anger just beneath the surface of his brother, but he'd never seen the immense brutality of it. Why the hell had he brought up Adam's dead mate?

Finally, Adam lifted off of him, breathing heavily, and

stood. Blood marred his knuckles, and Jasper knew his own face and arms wouldn't look much better.

"You will *never* bring up Anna again. You don't have the right. I lost *everything* because of those bastards, and yet I stood back and didn't retaliate because of my loyalty to this Pack. You let your mate walk out of your home without a fight because you were an ass and you hurt her. You are nothing. You don't deserve the power and station you wield nor do you deserve Willow. You better pray she is still alive. Because if anything has happened to her, I will kill you myself." Adam held out a hand. When Jasper gripped it, Adam hauled him to his feet.

"I will help you find her and bring her back. Not for you, but for her. With all that has happened in her life, she deserves happiness. Not a mate who would hold her back, for fear of his loss. And you will not force her to be with you. If she doesn't want you after this, because it is clear she left with a purpose, I will take care of her."

Jasper's wolf rose to the surface at the thought of his brother being with his mate.

His voice deepened to an almost growl. "You don't touch her."

"I don't want her sexually, you ass. But I will protect her like you should have. I don't want another mate. I've already been through that; I won't go through it again." Sadness and utter exhaustion covered Adam's features.

"Adam, I love her. She's everything to me."

"Then prove it. Once we find her, let her change. You both deserve it."

"I know that now."

"But you better do something to prove you deserve her. I won't let you hurt her again."

Reed came out of the darkness, anger evident on his features. "What the fuck are you two doing? You think fighting like a couple of asshats will solve anything?"

"Adam and I just needed to have a heart-to-heart. We're going."

"Good, because as the two of you waste time, the Centrals have your mate and you know it. Let's get going."

They ran to Reed's truck. As Jasper tried not to think about what could be happening to his Willow at this very moment. He prayed to God that his stupid, callous mistake didn't cost her her life.

Willow's breath came in shallow pants, waiting for Corbin's next move. After Hector's announcement of her imminent death, the prodigal son quickly removed her chains and carried her outside to a grass circle. The layout of stones reminded her somewhat of the Pack circle in the Redwood den. The pulsating magic of centuries of tradition she felt within the other circle calmed her. This one, however, held a sickly and fearful bitter after taste that made her skin crawl.

Her head lolling to the side, she blinked then stared down at the field below her. They had chained her to a wooden table in the center of the circle and angled it so she could see her surroundings. A blessing or a curse, she didn't know. The ground beneath her held a rusty hue, rather than the natural chestnut and tawny soil on the outskirts of the circle. Bile tried to worm its way up her throat as she tried to suppress the thoughts about what might have caused the dirty crimson overlay.

Another difference was, unlike the Redwood's circle, other than the three men corralling her, no others were present to bear witness to her torture. Her shame. Resigned to her fate, she prayed for quick death. Contrary to the Central's beliefs, Jasper wouldn't come for her. He'd told her he didn't want her, and she'd left. With every sneer and cruel promise from Hector and Corbin, Willow lost just a little bit more of who she was and what hope she could have held. A sense of loss and confusion enveloped her. No one would save her – not even herself.

Corbin's hand struck Willow's face. Hard. Pain shot through her cheek and jaw, as her eyes watered. She screamed, her voice breaking as she choked. She tried to squirm away, but the chains bit into her skin. After what seemed like hours, though it could only have been minutes from what Willow knew, Hector gave Corbin permission to begin his fun. She'd never thought she would miss the demented Alpha's crushing blows and slaps, but his son's ruthless and menacing smirk while he wielded his own punishment seeped into her soul and chipped away at her sanity. A fast end would surely be coming soon, right?

Hector stood in the center of the circle with an odd smile on his face. The demon, Caym, stood off to the side, also with a smile on his face. Though she could barely see it, as he continually looked off in the distance, his gaze on the outskirts of the circle. Like he waited for something, or someone, to come and interrupt their play at any moment. Her head hurt, and her thoughts had jumbled together. She closed her eyes, not aware of the others anymore.

The night had long since faded into the daylight hours. The cloudy overcast sky cast a sepia tone over the field, resembling an old picture. She tried to imagine she was just an observer, not a participant in this nightmare. A cool breeze brushed her skin, as Willow tried to forget where she was and focus on something else. Something more pleasant than the grueling pain inflicted by lunatic werewolves. Colorful, yet dead leaves fell to the ground in a gust of wind. Wasn't it an odd twist of fate that as leaves poetically withered and died their very essence would help create the pure beauty and elegance of the flora to come in the future? Would that happen to her when Corbin finally grew tired of his games? No, that wouldn't happen. She was just a human. A dying one.

"Willow, you aren't paying attention." Corbin's voice grated on her already frayed nerves, his anger oozing out in each syllable.

Corbin slapped her again. It hurt, yet the numbness from a constant attack settled over her. *Ah, sweet release.*

The light glistened on the tip of a knife he pulled out of his tool kit. Yes, the man actually had a tool kit for these special occasions. God help her. Her heart beat in a staccato pattern in her ear as he leaned over her body and smiled.

White, hot pain flashed in her side as he cut a shallow slice in her abdomen. He did it twice more as she screamed and cried. Corbin laughed and licked her blood from the knife. He moved his arms and the tip of his knife rested on her cheek. Willow froze in fear.

"I'm going to show that bastard pup you belong to me, if only for a little while." With a flick of his wrist, he dug the blade into her cheek. Salty tears pooled and slid down her face, mingling with her warm blood on her wind-cooled skin. If by some miraculous reason she survived this, she knew that final cut would scar her face for life.

Corbin stood, raising the knife above his head, and she flinched. He abruptly stopped lowering his arm. Instead of stabbing her, he threw back his head and laughed.

"Oh thank you for your fear. I relish in it."

He moved again, thrusting the knife toward her. She closed her eyes, ready for death.

The dull thunk of the blade embedding into the wooden table filled her ears.

Fucker keeps playing games.

He took her chin in his hand and forced her gaze to the knife buried to the hilt.

"That could have been you, my sweet. But I have been kind thus far." Corbin grinned with hooded eyes. "Not anymore."

Oh God.

He leaned over her head and strapped it to the table at an odd angle. "I won't bite you. No, you don't deserve the blessed gift that comes of my bite. But I will show you what it is like to marvel in the presence of a true wolf.

"You will never become a wolf. I will leave you here to die. And Jasper will come to find your rotting corpse. Too late to find the one he loved and lost."

"Jasper won't come for me." Her voice sounded rusty. She prayed Jasper would be safe from this tyrannical kingdom.

Corbin slapped her again and his palm connected with her cut. Though it stung a bit, she blessedly could hardly feel a thing.

"Oh, the fucker will. Believe me. Already they are on their way, though they have met our roadblocks. But those they fight are only our lower powered wolves that need to be culled. Once they get through that hurdle, he will be here."

God no. Please let him be lying.

"Even if Jasper doesn't love you, in truth, his wolf thinks you're his mate. Oh, Jasper will be forced, again, to try and save you, even if a whore like you doesn't deserve it. But his time he'll be too late."

Not Jasper. Corbin could do what he wished with her, but Jasper had to be safe.

"Now that I've secured your head to the table, if you close your eyes at all, I will prolong your suffering. Do you want that? No? I didn't think so."

He stood back and stripped himself of his clothing. Corbin howled then began the process of turning into his wolf. Willow watched as his muscles flexed and tore, and his bones broke and reformed. Fur sprouted from under his skin covering his body. His facial features lengthened; a muzzle and long canines dominated his face. Soon a midnight black wolf with chocolate brown paws stood beside her. She looked deep into his full black eyes. That's why they looked odd. Every other wolf she'd seen had a gold rim surrounding their normal eye color. Corbin's were a deep black, as if to swallow her soul along with killing her body.

Her breath hitched, and her pulse sped, beating in her ears. No tears fell from her eyes. She would not beg for her life. This cruel abomination of man was not worth it.

Corbin leapt toward her.

It really was a magnificent jump.

Claws ripped into her flesh, in a delayed reaction, she felt no pain. Caym moved into her field of vision and crooked a corner of his mouth into a grotesquely beautiful smile. A scream tore from her throat and the large tears in her flesh finally registered to her brain. He dug into her legs, stomach, arms. These weren't superficial cuts. She'd die. Soon.

Only her face, with the large cut from before, remained safe from his wrath. Excruciating agony filled her as she kept her eyes open. If she closed them, he would take longer. She didn't think she could last much longer anyway. Blood pooled around her body as black spots formed in her vision.

Jasper. I'm sorry. I never should've left. Forgive me.

Finally, his growls ceased as blessed darkness pulled her toward peace.

THE GROUND DUG into Willow's back. The air cool against her skin. A voice whispered in her ear. Willow didn't want to wake up. Why couldn't they leave her alone?

"Willow, wake up. You need to swallow this, it will help with the pain and aid with your healing. Please, wake up."

Willow opened her eyes and focused on the blurry image in front of her. Dark eyes and dark hair over smooth light mocha skin. Familiar. But who was she? Was she an angel? What happened? Why couldn't they leave her alone? She was dead.

She opened her mouth to speak but pain erupted in her head.

"Shh, don't try to speak. I'm Ellie, Corbin's sister. I'm here to help." She gave a sad smile and brushed the hair from Willow's face. "Please, drink." The woman named Ellie tipped the cup to her parched lips and forced a revolting, pickled liquid down her throat.

As soon as it hit her stomach, warmth radiated through her system and her blinding pain subsided.

Ellie set to removing some of her bindings and cleaned up some of the blood. How on earth was this kind and gentle woman related to those sadistic bastards? Tears streaked down the young woman's face as she pressed a cool cloth to Willow's cheek.

"I'm so sorry."

"Not your fault. Thank you." It hurt to speak, but whatever was in that cup had helped.

"Help is coming for you, Willow."

Willow just smiled and shook her head.

Ellie smiled back and kissed her forehead.

Finally, she fell back into a deep sleep. Maybe Ellie was right. Maybe Jasper would come after all.

18

Jasper tightened his jaw as his teeth sank into fur and flesh. He twisted his neck in a quick jerk, and the sound of his opponent's spine cracking in pieces echoed off the trees. The rust colored wolf grew limp, and he released him. The dead wolf fell to the ground among his compatriots. Foolish weak wolves thought they could fight against some of the top of the Redwood Pack.

When they'd first come upon the clearing, a group of fourteen low-ranking Centrals prowled among the trees on the outskirts of the forest, blocking their path. Jasper and his brothers calmly got out of the truck, as calm as they could be with tension and fury running through their veins, and changed into their wolves. As their animal counterparts, they bit, clawed, and attacked their way through the interfering wolves. With each strike, Jasper could only think of Willow. Was he too late? Would he reach her in time? What would he find when he got there?

Each minute that passed added another rock to the pile in his churning stomach of nerves. He called on his inner power and quickly shifted back to human, his brothers soon following.

"Shit, that was too easy." Reed was barely out of breath, as they all grabbed their clothing littered around the truck.

"I know. They were only a distraction. A delay." Anger burned in his veins. Those fuckers deserved their death. He wouldn't waste a moment of pity on their lifeless corpses. Hector and his son had his mate at this very moment. Nothing was more important that finding her. Saving her.

A lock of his hair brushed the back of his neck as the wind shifted. Something familiar tugged on his sense. Jasper inhaled. A faint trace of cinnamon.

Willow.

He threw back his head and howled, running through the trees, following the fading scent like a lifeline. He heard the gentle crunch of leaves behind him. His brothers followed, flanking him and protecting against unseen forces.

The familiar sickly sweet and tangy scent from before overlaid Willow's intoxicating cinnamon scent. Though it confirmed the connection between the Centrals and the murder of the Talon girl, Jasper could only think of running toward his Wil. Tree branches and stones cut his bare feet and arms as he hurried through the brush, keeping an eye on his surroundings.

"Find her."

Jasper didn't need his wolf's simply phrased demand to keep going. He could only pray she was alive. Only pray that she wasn't hurt. Too badly. The rumors concerning the Central Pack scared the shit out of him if they proved true with his Willow.

A branch scraped his cheek. Warm droplets of blood ran down his chin. He broke into the clearing.

Oh my God.

Willow lay prostrate on a wooden table, like a ruthless sacrifice to a god he would never know. A bloodied angel. Her brown hair flowed in the wind, giving her stilled body a ghostly movement.

Dark crimson pools fringed the table holding her. Burnt orange and yellow leaves adhered to the sticky substance in a cruel collage of pain and hatred. Chains lay on the ground, not attached to her. Someone had released her, but he couldn't think about that now. The dead grass of the circle looked like a wasteland of Pack culture and tradition, lacking the very essence of goodness and solidarity that made his Pack whole. No other sounds, breaths, and life signs remained, other than that of his brothers and, hopefully, his mate.

"Willow!"

A gut-wrenching scream ripped from his throat and he

forced his leaden limbs to action, running to her side. Blood pounded in his ears. The sound of Reed's shout of disbelief and Adam's cry of pain reached him. But Jasper couldn't focus on them.

He knelt by her side, tears streaking his face. Blood spattered almost every inch of her body. How on earth could one small human lose that much and still live? One large knife wound split her cheek. Slices and gashes covered her skin. Bile rose to this throat at the hint of muscles and organs though some of the deeper cuts.

Her chest rose and fell, slowly, raggedly. He exhaled in relief.

She was alive.

Thank God.

Careful not to touch anything that might hurt her, though it didn't look like that could be avoided, he caressed the clean side of her face. The coolness of her skin brought him out of his reverie.

"Willow." Though he meant his voice to carry and wake her, it came out on only a whisper.

"You must change her, Jasper." Adam's voice was a void of emotion.

Not an option.

"I can't, Adam. Do you know what I would have to do? I can't hurt her any more than she already is. My wolf won't allow it." As it was, his wolf whimpered, struggling not to curl next to its mate and pray.

"Jasper, we can't do it. We don't have that kind of power. Only you, Kade, and Dad do." Reed's voice broke.

"It has to be you, Jasper. You need to be the one who changes her. Only you can save her." Adam's voice held no pity in his voice, only strength of acceptance.

Sobs wracked his body as he gained the courage to do what must be done.

God, I promise that I will leave her alone or do whatever she needs, but please, let her be okay. Don't let my foolish mistake of careless words and not being able to protect her take her life. Please.

He took a steadying breath and stood to strip out of his clothes. His brothers gave him an encouraging nod, and Jasper called his power, to change into his wolf. It took precious energy from him every time he forced the change, but only his determination to save his mate gave him the strength.

When he changed, he padded to his mate's side and licked her face, whimpering at her wounds. He couldn't be the man during this, so he let his wolf come to the surface, relishing the power and animalistic sense of cohesiveness. Almost like watching through a haze, he sobbed and nuzzled Willow.

Around him, Adam and Reed checked the perimeter, then knelt to hold Willow down, just in case by some twist of fate, she moved or struggled during the transformation.

He huffed out a breath, nuzzled her one more time, then bit the fleshly part of her arm.

A rush of pain through their shallow bond and a trickle of blood.

This was not a hunt and his final catch of his prey. No, this was his mate. He released her arm and bit into her shoulder, growling in fury. This shouldn't be him. But it was his penance. Only a small piece of it. She was in this situation because of him. Though with each bite and tear a small piece of him died, it would not be enough. Nothing he did would compensate for the fact she lay practically dead due to his words.

He bit again and again and, with each bite, released more of the enzyme that made them who they were. He prayed it took. Just a small amount of the enzyme wouldn't do. It had to take.

A shaking hand on his back stopped him.

"That should be enough, Jasper," Reed choked.

With tear-filled eyes, Adam knelt and placed Jasper's jacket over her still form. Thank God he used his and not Adam's. Though he might not deserve it, the possessiveness of his wolf wouldn't allow another male to scent her. His brother knelt and carefully picked her up, holding her to his chest like fine china.

Jasper used his remaining energy to change back to human and tugged on his clothes, weariness dissolving into his bones. He walked toward Adam, hands outstretched for his mate.

Adam softly growled and shook his head, while Reed tried to step between them. What the fuck?

"Adam, now is not the time to push my buttons. Hand her to me. I need her." Need was such a weak word compared to what he felt.

His wolf growled in agreement.

"You must earn her trust back, Jasper. Do you really think you deserve to hold her?" His brother's chest heaved in growing anger.

What the hell? Did Adam really think it was okay to hold his mate hostage? He might have made the worst mistake of his life letting her walk out of their home, but Jasper needed her by his side.

"Adam, give me my mate. My wolf needs her to calm. And let's not forget that another spirit is melding itself to her right as we speak. She needs me. I need her. She's my everything."

Adam begrudgingly sighed then gently placed Willow into the cradle of Jasper's arms. Her cool weight settled on him like a long lost limb. Rightness. He brought her closer, inhaling her cinnamon scent. Their heartbeats synching into their familiar steady and living rhythm.

"When she wakes up, she gets a choice. This is not your decision," Adam growled.

Jasper nodded, without taking his eyes off her. Oh, he

would give her the choice he should have from the beginning. But he would use every ounce of himself to prove his worth. His love.

Not a word left their lips on the trip back to the truck. Careful not to jar her injuries, yet hesitant to linger any longer in enemy territory, Jasper walked softly, whispering words of faith and hope to her.

As soon as they reached their home, North burst from the front door, his serious doctor face on. Thank God for his brother's medical skills. He might not be the true Healer of the Pack, but his hands held mercy and a healing power of their own.

Jasper held off his brother, in too much pain to let go of Willow even for the walk up the steps. His father and Kade stood in his living room, anxious and grieved expressions on their faces.

A muffled scream brought his attention to the bedroom doorway. His mother stood with one hand clasped over her mouth, the other on her chest.

"She's alive, Mom."

She nodded then walked hesitantly toward Willow.

"Someone has begun the healing process."

"I know. I scented a potion of some sort on her when we got there. I don't even want to think about what she looked like before."

"Jasper," North whispered, "we need to get her to the bedroom so I can make sure she's healing okay. I can already tell that some things are already healing, as some of these cuts have become smaller in the last two minutes, but I need to examine her.

Jasper walked past his family, into the bedroom and placed her in the center of the bed, watching as her wounds sealed. It had taken. *She'd change at the next moon. Thank God.* If only he'd have said okay to the transformation before. There was no doubt in his mind what she'd gone through far surpassed any pain and agony she would have endured in a sterile change, such as Mel's.

And it was his fault.

North and his mother set to work, cleaning off the blood, dirt, and gore while checking her vitals. Not needed, and feeling deservingly unwanted, Jasper walked back to the living room.

"She's going to be okay." Though his voice broke, he did not cry. Not now. He had to be strong for her, even though inside he was crumbling.

"I don't know how you did it, bro," Kade wondered aloud. "I could barely handle being in the same room when Dad changed Mel. How could you do that to Willow?"

"I had to, Kade. There was no one else. What else could I do? But, yes, I will have to live with the fact that, not only did I cause her to be there, I had to be the one who changed her." Shudders racked his body, remembering the taste of her blood on his tongue. *Never again.*

"I hope, son, that it will be enough power." His father's

voice wrapped around him like an old blanket. "After going through so many changes and then having only a Beta to force the change, it will be tricky."

"It has to be enough." There was no other choice.

"Though she's healing now, there's no guarantee she will wake up. Or that she will survive the first change." Reed's statement was an unwelcome reminder of the tenuous nature of their race.

He left the room and returned to the bedroom while they discussed the ramifications of the Central's attack and what must be done. Though it was also his job, he couldn't focus on it. His sole reason for living lay prone on their bed, struggling to live.

North sat in a chair beside the bed, watching the rise and fall of her chest. Next to him, on the nightstand, the wooden angel figurine Jasper had made for Willow, stood vigil, her oak palms in prayer. He'd made it for her as a present, but had yet to give it to her. His mother scurried around the room, cleaning up the blood-soaked sheets and cloths, a determined look on her face. His mother was no wilting flower. No, royal werewolf blood ran through her veins, her pride in her heritage evident in the way she held her head high and had raised her family. It had also shown in how she took care of her Pack.

Jasper knelt on the floor next to Willow, taking in her gaunt features. Even pale, with the new scar on her cheek, beauty emanated from her skin, her soul. He closed his eyes and prayed.

Dear Lord, please let her live. Let her survive the change. She doesn't deserve anything that has happened to her. She gave up everything to be part of this Pack. Don't let her give her life as well. She can hate me with every fiber of her being, as long as she wakes. I'll do anything for her, even walk away. But, please, save her.

With a final thanks for her survival, Jasper opened his eyes and leaned over her to kiss her scarred cheek. Yes, no matter what, he would show her what she meant to him. To the Pack. He only hoped she could forgive him. Because he would never forgive himself.

19

The lingering smell of sandalwood tickled Willow's nose. She inhaled, letting the familiar and, for some reason, loving scent, bring her closer to the surface of the deep pool she swam in. Floating higher and higher, she basked in the soothing warmth, wrapping around her like an old friend.

"Wake up, Willow. Open your eyes. It's time to begin."

Who was that?

The soft feminine voice didn't sound like anyone she knew. Wait, who did she know? Where was she?

Questions formed and tumbled in her mind, cooling the surrounding warmth as she tried to make sense of what was happening.

The sounds of footsteps on the lush carpet mingled with the crunching of grass beneath a person's foot. The bending of a blade of grass underneath a paw sounded crisp and clean. So near. A door opened to a home, followed by more footsteps.

Behind the intense sandalwood came the strong scent of freshly ground coffee, fatty bacon sizzling in a pan, the creamy scent of homemade pancakes with fresh whipped cream and berries. The sharp citrus smell of squeezed orange juice overpowered her senses as she caught a whiff of wood shavings.

Why could she hear and smell all of this? What was going on?

Willow steadied herself and cracked open her eyes. Blinding light flooded her eyes, and she quickly closed them. A throaty moan escaped her lips, as she repeated the painful process again.

Was this bright light heaven?

Was she truly dead?

A figure sat beside where she lay. She squinted to clarify the image.

Adam.

Disappointment swelled. Why had she thought Jasper would be next to her when she woke? *If* she woke. Obviously, she was nothing to him. Adam being here proved that.

"Willow?" Her brother-in-law's voice was barely a whisper, as though shocked to see her alive. At least that was what she thought, though it could be about what she looked like. Because if she looked like how she felt, then a pile of dirty laundry and rocks would be a step up right about now.

She tried to swallow, but her throat was too dry.

Adam placed a cup of cool water on her lips and she drank greedily. The gesture was so different from when Corbin had done the same when he held her captive, nearly drowning her in the process. It wasn't, however, the same as if Jasper had done it.

"Jasper?"

Dammit. She hadn't wanted to say that. Didn't want to show the world how much he still meant to her.

Adam smiled.

"He's sleeping on the couch. Took all I had in me to force him to sleep. He's been by your side for the four days you've been out. Watching you breathe, making sure you were as comfortable as possible."

"Four days?" How bad was she if she'd been out for *four* days?

"Yeah, Wil. You were down for the count." He smiled again and looked relived. "Thank God you're awake now."

"Who was the woman? You only mentioned you and Jasper in the house, but I heard a woman's voice telling me to wake up. Who was here?"

He looked confused. "It's only been me and Jasper for three days, Wil. We didn't want to overwhelm you. We wanted to give you time to wake up, to heal. No woman has been here."

"I'm your wolf, dear. Get used to me."

Holy crap.

"I'm a werewolf."

Adam smiled a sad smile, nodding. "Yes, Wil. That you are."

"Willow."

The sound of Jasper's awe-filled, raspy voice in the doorway forced her to turn toward him.

It looked as if he hadn't slept in days. Tired lines circled his haunted eyes. Was it because he'd seen what happened to her? Had he missed her?

Jasper looked guilty and sad, but every time she felt the burn in her chest from taking too deep a breath, her body ached. Old tears streaked his face and she knew she would forgive him for his words—eventually. He wasn't the one who'd gutted her. No, that had been those sadistic bastards Corbin and Hector. She tried to remember exactly what had happened, but only fuzzy memoires came to the surface.

She wanted him to come to her and hold her until she felt better. To make her feel whole again and help with her overwhelming senses. But then, she also wanted to kick his ass and throw him out of the room. Her dumbass male thought it was okay to think it was all about him and his choices?

Bastard.

Well, it was too late now, wasn't it? The wolf that whispered to her to love Jasper proved Jasper had been wrong and she could survive the bite. She *had* survived the bite. The contradicting thoughts and desires were no help to her already muddled brain.

Jasper stood in the doorway, hesitant to walk into the room. She could smell the worry and hope wafting off his skin. *Weird.* He clenched his fists, rocking on the balls of his feet, as though he were ready to spring into the room at a moment's notice. His worn jeans clung to his legs, and a wrinkled T-shirt stretched tight across his muscles brought a need to her she didn't want to think about.

Mate.

Was this what he dealt with every day? Why he was also so primal toward her during their lovemaking?

Not sure what I think about that.

"What happened, Jasper?" If he wasn't going to step into the room, well then she needed some answers.

He opened his mouth to speak, but Adam cut him off.

"What do you remember, Willow?"

Images flashed through her mind. A dark bedroom, then a wooden table. A cold glint of metal. Warm blood seeping from her pores. Slicing pain racking her body. Flashes of agony. Ghostly feelings that would never fade.

An inhuman whine escaped from her throat. She closed her eyes to try and block out the memories.

"Everything will be okay, Willow. Together, we are strong. And our mate is here."

She didn't want to rely on her mate. Look where that got

her. Stupid new wolf didn't know anything. And frankly, she wasn't sure if Jasper even wanted her to be with him to begin with.

Her body ached when she tried to move, and a sharp pain stabbed in her side. Adam quickly put his hand on her arm to settle her. She whimpered again at the feel of his touch. No, this wasn't right. He wasn't hers and not what she needed.

Jasper growled from the doorway and rushed to her side. As soon as he neared, his mere presence calmed her wolf. *Idiot wolf. She wasn't supposed to feel for the man who didn't really love her.* If the damn thing had been a cat, she surely would've purred in contentment. *Annoying.*

Adam raised an eyebrow and released her arm, backing away slowly. He gave a nod to them both, and then retreated from the room, closing the door softly behind him. But from what she could tell from her newly enhanced senses, a closed door wouldn't stop him from listening in. However, the green eyes assessing her every feature put all thoughts of Adam out of her mind.

Jasper slid onto the bed, careful not to jar her body and cause her pain. How frustrating. He wasn't supposed to be nice and cautious of her well-being. He was supposed to hate her. How else would she have ended up in this situation?

"Willow, baby. I'm so sorry."

Tears filled her eyes. His admission didn't change the fact that she hurt. Everywhere.

"I didn't mean what I said," Jasper whispered. "I only meant that because you knew me, the Centrals wanted you. Not that *I* didn't want you."

Warmth filled her chest. Could she believe him? What if he changed his mind? Again. Could she really be that girl who waited for her husband, without something of her own? She didn't want to be worthless, depending on others, lacking a purpose.

"This was all my fault, Willow. I shouldn't have denied you your choices. I love you. I'm so happy that you're my mate and we are bound. But I wish the circumstances were different. That's what I could have said. Not mumbled my displeasure at others."

Hope cascaded through her, but she ignored it. She wasn't ready to trust him yet.

"I wanted you, Jasper. I've wanted you since you walked through my bakery door asking for cinnamon rolls." Her voice lowered, unsure.

"And I'm an idiot. You deserve a lifetime of happiness and are going to make a beautiful wolf. I shouldn't have let my fears step in the way of what you mean to me. I'm so sorry."

Tears fell down his cheeks, splashing the bedspread.

"I'm so sorry you got hurt and almost killed because of me."

Though he held some of the guilt on his shoulders, she couldn't allow him to carry it all.

"Jasper, it isn't your fault. I shouldn't have left the house and walked outside in the dark with a killer on the loose. Why don't you just slap a 'kill the dumb chick' sign on my forehead?"

"You weren't thinking clearly because of what I said. Don't take the blame for that."

"Fine, but that means you can't either. I can blame you for saying what you said, but not for me getting kidnapped and almost killed. No, that wasn't you. That was the Centrals. They were the ones who tortured me. Not you. I got hurt because those men are sadistic wolves who thrive on the pain and powerless feelings of others. They got someone to take me from my home." Her voice trembled.

A familiar, yet unrecognizable face flashed in her mind and a sharp pain radiated in her temples.

"What do you mean? Who took you? Do you remember?" Jasper's voice rose slightly.

Just as quickly as it came, the image faded away. *Damn.*

"I can't remember exactly. But something's there. I know it." Frustration clawed at her as she tried to latch onto a memory.

"Take your time. It will come to you."

She sighed. If only it would come now, rather than later. That way she could put it behind her.

"I want you to know that you can do anything you want

once you get better. I'll do anything you want. You just need to heal."

What the hell was he talking about? Where was her strong-willed mate? Did he really feel that bad? She missed his Beta attitude.

"I don't want to do anything else. Stop blaming yourself."

He sighed. "Just get healthy."

"I guess I have a long time to be healthy now."

Jasper let out a watery laugh and leaned over to brush his lips lightly against hers. Her wolf howled at the contact. What an odd feeling, having another spirit sharing her space, feeling her moods and touches. She did agree with her wolf that his lips were soft and brought a needy feeling in her.

When he lifted his lips after the brief sweet kiss, his eyes widened. A slow smile crept over his face.

"I think my wolf likes yours. This could be interesting, watching them preen for each other."

Oh yes, very interesting.

"I forgive you, Jasper."

He stopped moving, and his smile fell from his face.

"Willow, don't you need more time?"

She smiled. "Shut up, Jasper. I forgive you. We need to move on, and I need your help. Kiss me again." She liked this more assertive side of hers. Maybe this werewolf thing won't be too bad.

"See, I told you I'm pretty awesome. You'll see the magnitude of my greatness."

Willow smiled at her wolf's cute attitude. It would take some getting used to, but totally do-able.

Jasper smiled and kissed her again. His lips parted and her tongue darted into his mouth. That sandalwood scent enveloped her, wrapping her in a cocoon. His sweet taste burst on her taste buds. *Dear God, did Jasper always taste this orgasmic?* She loved being a wolf. She tried to reach for him to urge him to continue, but he pulled back and kissed her forehead.

"You need your rest and I don't want you to overexert yourself. I'll be here when you wake up." He smiled, and she fell for him again. He left the room, closing the door as quietly as Adam had.

Yes, she loved him and forgave him. But that niggling feeling wouldn't go away. Could she trust him? She just didn't know.

"That's a foolish way to look at it. He's our mate."

Her wolf was too young to know what she was talking about.

"Hey I may be new to you, but that doesn't mean I'm young."

Huh?

"You're tired. I'll tell you all about spirits and the Moon Goddess later. But you can trust Jasper."

She so wanted to believe that. But she'd followed her heart blindly before and look at the pain it caused. No, it would take time and action rather than faith to find a new balance in their relationship.

JASPER WALKED BACK into the room twenty minutes later to check on her. Willow lay under the covers, sleeping soundly with a small smile on her face. The cuts and bruises had healed fully the day before, but she would still be sore. Too sore for his comfort. And what would come tonight wouldn't help her soreness. Because tonight the full moon rose high in the sky, the first time she would change – if she could change without dying in the process. He quickly buried those useless thoughts. They would only bring more pain, more grief.

Though werewolves didn't need the full moon to change, their initial change always occurred on their first full moon. Whether they were changed as adults or sometime after their third birthday, the moon would call. And those with strong enough bodies would answer.

Jasper sat on a chair next to the bed. In his hands, he held a piece of fine oak, smooth and ready to be molded. An outline of a female wolf began to take shape. He took his carving knife, slowly adding details and intricacies of what she could look like as a wolf. Once Willow changed, he would add an exact likeness. The wood felt warm in his hands. Heavy. Substantial. Something he had the power to change and control. Though the grains of wood would voice their desires, Jasper's expert hands could form what he wanted. What he needed. Not the case for the woman in front of him.

Her cinnamon scent filled his nostrils, calming him. She was safe. At least for the moment. Her scent now held traces of wolf, hidden among her original scent. It was sexy as hell. Once she changed, the scent would only intensify.

He'd almost lost her.

Blissful relief spread through him at that one word: almost.

Her wolf would be beautiful. He could already sense her spirit. The new wolf felt strong and would be able to carry Willow through anything. Already a strong woman, her new addition would only increase her power. And if she allowed him by her side, she could face anything. He would be damn sure she had the defenses to do so.

The choice would be hers, though he didn't know what he would do if she walked away. And God forbid if she found another male. When Adam had touched her earlier, flames burst through his skin and seeped into his bones. He thought he would jump across the room and punch his little brother square in the face, but he fought the urge. When she'd whimpered at that touch, he'd almost torn Adam's arm from his body.

He would stand by and let her walk away from him if that was her choice. It needed to be her choice, though it would tear him to pieces and destroy his soul to do so. He knew she said she'd forgiven him, but he'd seen something in her eyes when she said it.

She might forgive him, but she didn't trust him.

He would do anything to regain that trust.

20

———————

Willow took a deep breath and gripped the wooden dresser to hide her shaking fingers. Her body was still sore, but she was still surprised at the lack of bruises covering her skin. This new healing ability was sure something. A light caught her eyes in the reflection, and she jumped.

Gold.

A werewolf. A mere human no more. And tonight she'd find out if she could handle the change. She closed her eyes, not wanting to look at the reminder that her life as she knew it was forever changed. Over.

Now she'd walk on four legs under the moonlight and howl to their goddess. Hunt for prey and open her senses. She stood naked in front of the mirror, trying to calm her nerves before her first hunt. Her first change. The full moon called to her, tugged at her bones, seeped in her pores, her blood.

Jasper said it would hurt. He wouldn't lie to her. Not now. But he qualified it with sad eyes and said it wouldn't be as bad as what she already went through. Not nearly as bad.

She shuddered.

Thank God.

She put her arms through one of Jasper's soft flannel shirts and buttoned it up. They'd be naked before the shift but didn't want to walk about in her birthday suit just yet. And, if she were honest with herself, she wanted to envelop herself in her mate's scent.

She held the long sleeves up to her nose and inhaled.

Oh, how she missed him.

"He will protect you tonight, Willow. Always. Forgive him."

It was still so weird to hear another person, albeit a wolf, sharing her mind. But, she didn't know if she could fully agree with her wolf – yet. Time would tell.

"Are you ready to go, Wil?" Jasper cautiously walked toward her.

Clad in only sweat pants, his bare chest begged for her hands. But she shook it off. Too soon. Way too soon.

She nodded, not knowing what else to say. Fear choked her. Why was she so afraid? She wanted this. Besides, she'd been through worse. But this time was different. She was going to change into a being that gave people nightmares. She loved Jasper's wolf. The feel of his fur against her skin, his warm body leaning against hers as he panted from exertion from his runs.

She could do this. This was her destiny.

She squared her shoulders and took his hand. He jumped at the contact and gave her a small smile.

Jesus, he looked so guilty. So pained. He hadn't hurt her physically, just emotionally. And even then, she knew why he'd said it. He was just a stupid male, not the sadistic bastard Corbin was.

"Come on, let's get wolfy." She smiled.

Jasper cut off a laugh and shook his head. "Okay then."

He led her toward the backyard facing the alcove of trees. The wind brushed her hair, ticking her nose. It would only be the two of them tonight. She didn't need the Alpha, as it was Jasper, not Edward, who bit her enough times to bring on the change and call to her wolf spirit. She only needed to be by his side and call forth her wolf under her first full moon. They would meet up with the others for the rest of the hunt after she changed. If she changed.

A shudder ran through her. She was so scared, yet Jasper was her rock. He showed no fear and helped her. But she knew inside it must be different, that he felt the same fear she did.

He turned her around to face him once they reached the center of their yard. He slowly unbuttoned her shirt, and she let out a gasp.

Oh my.

His calloused fingertips brushed against her skin as the moonlight danced upon it. She inhaled the clean, crisp mountain air that mingled with Jasper's sandalwood scent.

Home.

Yes, that is what this felt like. What could be wrong with this? Though it may not seem right, and not inherent to nature, she knew the change was right for her. Inherent to her being. No amount of pain would take her away from this. This was hers.

Soon she stood naked in the moonlight and her skin began to itch, like something was coming or missing. She didn't know, but she knew her wolf would tell her.

"Willow, babe? I will hold on to you during your first shift." She relaxed slightly at Jasper's words. "You will change in my arms, and I won't let you go until you are a wolf. Then I will shift beside you. Okay?"

She nodded then the first burst of pain racked her body and she let out a whimper.

"Shh." Jasper pulled her in his arms, resting her head on his naked chest.

Another whimper turned to a scream as pain shot down her body.

"It will be okay Willow. It's only natural".

"Natural? Really?" She said to her wolf.

Jasper merely lifted a brow at her nonsensical words, and a blush covered her naked body.

"You'll get used to talking to your wolf. I do it all the time." He gave her a small smile.

Sharp pinpricks of pain danced along her spine, and she bowed into his arms. He pulled her closer to his chest and she inhaled his scent and relaxed. Jasper lowered them to the ground, cradling her in his arms, and kissed her deeply. Their tongues clashed and mated, bringing Willow's thoughts to him and his sensual taste, rather than concentrating on the pain racking her body.

Wow, love that type of distraction.

Jasper pulled his lips away and whispered, "I will be here. Always."

She smiled then screamed as her bones broke and her muscles tore.

Oh, God. How did Jasper do this daily?

Tears ran down her cheeks and her body molded and reformed. Fur sprouted along her skin, and her facial muscles went numb then cracked and reformed. Her vision blurred, then came back crisper. Clearer. She screamed once more as her body made its final painful alteration, and she ended on a howl. She bent her head and looked at her paws. Paws?

She was a wolf.

Holy crap.

"Wow, you've got to be the most beautiful wolf I've ever seen," Jasper rasped.

If a wolf could blush, she was sure she'd be doing it at

the moment. But instead, she just rolled her eyes. That seemed like a universal trait to tell a man he was full of it.

He laughed and pet her fur. Her fur. How crazy. She leaned into his touch, loving the way his hands felt on her over-heated skin beneath her pelt. An odd sensation for sure, but totally amazing.

She rolled her neck, needing some room to get used to her new body, and Jasper released her. She maneuvered herself to stand on all four paws, loving the way the grass felt between her claws. Jasper stood and smiled down on her. Cautiously, she walked toward him.

Well, at least she tried.

One back paw collided with a front paw, and she landed face first in the dirt, a collage of legs and fur.

She looked up at her mate holding back a laugh.

This is so *not funny.*

Okay, maybe a little. But he didn't have to laugh about it.

"Baby, you'll get used to it. I promise." Jasper chuckled.

Willow tilted her head. *Really?*

"Hey, I was a pup when I learned to walk on four paws. I'm sure I ate dirt a few times. You should ask North about the time he learned. I swear, for a doctor who now has such great reflexes, as a kid, he had horrible balance issues. But really, Willow, let your wolf come forward. She'll teach you what you need to know."

"I'll help, don't worry. You'll have control, but I will aide you."

Willow relaxed with both their encouragements. At least she didn't feel completely alone in this.

Jasper took off his sweats, and he stood gloriously naked, his erection jutting out.

He gave a small, sheepish smile. "Sorry, you were naked. I couldn't help it."

What did he have to be sorry about? She only wished she were human so she could jump his bones.

She panted at the thought.

Her wolf laughed. *"You can do that later. Enjoy your hunt. And no, we don't do the nasty in our wolf forms. Some lines you just don't cross."*

Willow let out a grunt that sounded like a laugh.

She watched as her mate turned to a magnificent black wolf, and came at her, nipping playfully at her legs and flank. He licked her muzzle and she bent into him, inhaling his scent.

"Sexy wolf."

Willow totally agreed with her wolf.

Jasper nudged her, and Willow let go of her control. Her wolf sprang forward in her mind, and her body followed suit. She ran through the forest, the grass and dirt crunching beneath the pads of her paws. Low-lying branches brushed her flank, but she leapt out of their way and over fallen logs at a fast pace. She quickened as she went up a hill, stopping once she reached the top. Jasper came to a stop behind her, and she howled at the moon, knowing full well she was fitting into a stereotype. But why the hell not?

Jasper joined her in her howl, his deep baritone blending with her softer pitch. Together their music was a melody of unity, passion, and love.

Her mate.

For always.

LATER, still in wolf form, Jasper and Willow ran through the forest to meet up with the others. The overwhelming scents of other wolves assaulted her nose and she shook her muzzle. It was still so weird to get used to seeing so many werewolves in one place, snuggling, exploring, and yipping. Like a family. A large hairy one.

A big gray wolf entered the clearing, and the slight growls and yips quieted. She recognized this wolf. Edward.

Their Alpha.

Her Alpha.

Without knowing why she did it, other than it was an inherent part of her, a calling, she lowered her body in submission, tilting her head to bare her throat to Edward.

The Alpha padded toward her and locked his jaw around her throat, using a light pressure to show her who was in charge. Her wolf relaxed as a sense of being – of rightness – settled over her.

She was Pack in truth.

Home.

Edward released her and howled. The surrounding wolves joined in. Jasper nudged her flank, and then licked the spots where Edward's scent lingered, effectively staking his claim as well. Though the human in her might still be cautious toward him, her wolf felt comforted by his gesture and leaned into his touch. Jasper lifted his head and howled with his family, Willow joining in soon after.

As if an unheard signal went off, the wolves began their hunt. The younger pups, adorable on their new legs and soft fur, stayed close to their mothers, as their fathers ran off with the men to hunt. Though it might have seemed barbaric to her, she felt the ancient customs of men providing for their family was comforting to her wolf. When she saw a smaller wolf dart off with the larger ones, Willow almost laughed. Cailin joined the men, hunting her prey. Those poor men.

The thumping of small feet reached her ears.

A rabbit.

A juicy, mouthwatering rabbit.

Her wolf perked up, and she was off, running after the sound, using the instincts she didn't know she possessed. Another small wolf ran by her side.

Mel.

Together, the two women, now sisters, gave chase. Willow hunkered down up wind, and waited, Mel doing the same by her side. The large rabbit hopped into a clear view, and Willow nudged Mel.

Mel nodded. Then pounced.

Willow was still new at this, but this was Mel's third time on the hunt.

Together they killed their dinner and sat, tongues wagging, at their good fortune.

If wolves could laugh, she was sure Jasper was doing so when he walked to her side, Kade right behind him walking toward Mel. He dropped another, larger, rabbit by her feet and used his muzzle to scoot it toward her.

Aww. How sweet. He got me a meal.

Too bad she was a strong female werewolf and could provide for herself. But it was the thought that counted.

Wow, times sure have changed.

She bit into the rabbit and grimaced. Her wolf liked it, but geez. This was like the Easter bunny or something.

Just imagine it's a chocolate-filled one. Yeah that will work. Not.

After the four of them ate, Kade licked Mel's face then nodded toward them, gesturing toward the woods. Jasper gave a small growl, and the other couple ran back into the forest, leaving her and Jasper alone in the clearing.

She stretched her mouth in a wide yawn, though she wasn't that tired. Jasper nipped her side then covered her smaller body to protect her while she changed back.

Once human, she sat naked on the grass, under the trees, feeling invigorated.

Jasper changed back to human, and she panted with need. He crooked a brow and opened his mouth to speak, but she grabbed his cock and pulled him closer instead.

"Jesus, Willow," he grunted.

He crushed his mouth to hers, her taste bursting on his tongue. She growled into his mouth, licking his tongue and nipping at his lips. Blood pumping, she couldn't get enough of him. She needed him. Now.

He thrust into her fist, growling. She moaned when he squeezed her rear, pulling her closer.

Jasper pulled away, fire and caring in his eyes. "We should get back to our clothes. I don't want you to get sick. You just got well."

Damn her mate and his seeing to her needs. She needed this first.

Willow shook her head. "After." She didn't know if this brazen part of herself was due to her wolf or the fact that Jasper was the sexiest man she'd ever seen, but she didn't care. She wanted him inside her. Soon.

Jasper groaned. "No complaints from me." He thrust his cock into her closed hand, increasing the friction, and moved his hand to play with her lower lips, soaking him.

"Jesus," she rasped as he inserted two fingers into her, curling them to rub on her most sensitive spot.

"You like that? You did so well today, baby. You were such a fucking fantastic wolf. You deserve a reward." The wicked gleam in his eyes almost made her come on the spot.

He pulled out of her reach and kissed her once more, before turning her.

"Seeing you as your wolf put a thought in my mind." He put her on all fours, her knees sinking into the wet soil.

She screamed when he licked her seam all the way to her clit. He grabbed both cheeks and spread her. The cool breeze felt like heaven against her overheated sensitive flesh. Jasper growled then buried his face, sucking and nibbling her.

She buckled and leaned back, urging him to go deeper.

His tongue darted in and out, then he bit down on her clit. She called his name, and before her mind could clear from the earth shattering orgasm, Jasper mounted her in one stroke.

He filled her completely, body and soul. He reared back and thrust again, his balls slapping her swollen pussy as he did it again. Together, they healed. Their souls combining, their bond tightening. Whatever had happened in the past was just that – the past. Everything was forgiven and they were ready to move forward.

He gripped her hips with a bruising force and swiveled his hips, hitting her just right. One more stroke and they came together in a connection of bliss.

Jasper pulled out of her, turned her to her back, then kissed her deeply.

"I love you," he whispered.

"I love you, too."

He lifted her up, a playful and dangerous glee in his eyes, and wrapped her legs around his hips, placing her back against the tree. The bark dug into her skin, the pain feeling soft and good.

Jasper smiled then entered her. Hard. Her core, already swollen and wet, clenched around him. He smiled and stopped where he was. He released one hand to brush the hair from her face, a smile on his lips.

This was perfection.

This was her mate.

Jasper reared back and slowly entered her again, rotating his hips to brush her clit. His strokes stayed steady and purposeful, but they never broke eye contact. Finally, she blinked and smiled.

"Let me mark you," she whispered.

Unsurpassed pleasure flashed over his face. "Make me yours."

She leaned forward, her fangs elongated, and bit into the soft spot where his shoulder met his neck. They came together with his shout as she pressed down harder, marking him as her mate.

Forever.

21

"Okay, what about this one?" Jasper laughed as he placed it near her lips.

Willow sat on the counter, her legs spread, his body between them. He'd blindfolded her with a silk tie and kissed her gently while he did it.

"Um, a cucumber?" She giggled.

Lord, his mate was too cute for her own good.

"What the hell does a cucumber smell like?"

"Well, like a cucumber. And green." She smiled and he leaned over to kiss her soft lips.

"Baby, I hate to be the one to tell you this, but green doesn't smell. Even to a werewolf."

"Hey, don't take away my fun. If I say it smells green, it smells green." She stuck out her lip like Marilyn Monroe, giving Jasper the urge to bite it.

Knowing he couldn't distract their lessons with sex – though it did sound like a fantastic idea, if he did say so himself – he just laughed instead.

"Hey, shut it. Don't laugh at me. Cucumber green smells green. Was I right?"

"Yes, yes. It was a cucumber. Your nose is amazing. You are werewolf perfect. But you are weird, but that's why I love you."

"Well, Jasper, you're the one teaching me. What did you expect?"

Oh, that was it.

He grabbed her waist, tickling her. Willow wiggled, trying to get away, laughing. They were in the kitchen, teaching her the ability to home in on a scent. Through the past week, he'd slowly taught her what it meant to be a werewolf. She wouldn't be in top form for a while yet, but she was improving remarkably. But it didn't surprise him. She was his mate after all.

The door opened behind them, but he continued his torture on Willow. He'd heard Adam coming up the steps; no doubt Willow did as well. But, geez, at some point his family would have to learn to knock.

"Whew, thank God you two are dressed. I so didn't need to see that. Again." Adam laughed.

He felt her blood rush to the surface as it lay against his skin. Yeah, that time on the kitchen table had really embarrassed her, but damn, it had been totally worth it.

Willow jumped off the counter, removed her blindfold, and jumped into Adam's arms in a huge hug. She was like that with all his family. At first it made him jealous as hell, but now he loved it. It meant she felt at home with him and his life, that she felt comfortable enough to be herself. She and Adam were closer than the rest, forming a friendship over her kidnapping and his loss of Anna. He felt a twinge of jealousy at it, but shook it off. Willow hadn't left him yet, and he hoped she never would. She said she'd forgiven him and they were closer than ever. But did she really trust him?

"Um, are you sure I wasn't interrupting?" Adam asked, a brow raised and bent down.

The blindfold dangling on his finger caused both men to laugh.

"Hey." Willow playfully hit both of them. "It's not what it looks like. We were just practicing."

They laughed harder.

If Willow blushed any harder, she'd be Santa red.

"I meant," she began smoothly, "we were practicing with scents."

Jasper tugged her close and kissed the crown of her head. "It's fine, baby. We were just joking. But, Adam, was there a particular reason you were here? Or just to show your ugly face?"

"Ouch, man. That hurt. I brought some papers and deeds for you that need your John Hancock."

Ahh, the joys of being a Beta. Jasper sighed. He loved his

work, taking care of and protecting his Pack, but the paperwork in this modern society was a bitch. And frankly, he'd hoped Adam was here with news from the Centrals. But that never seemed to be the case. The bastards had gone underground. There wasn't a trace of Hector or Corbin. Anger coursed his veins and he clenched his jaw.

Warm lips caressed his chin. "Hey, stop scowling."

Jasper nipped at her fingers and growled. "Sorry."

"Hey, I can leave if you want."

Crap, forgot Adam was still there.

Jasper cleared his throat. "No, stay. Really, we were just hanging out. Promise."

Adam shrugged.

"Please?" Willow asked. "I made Greek salad, baba ganoush, and chocolate baklava. And I brought fresh bread from the bakery on my way home."

Adam groaned. "Sounds amazing. But, where's the meat?"

Jasper laughed. That's what he was thinking.

Willow let out a laugh. "You could get over it, Adam. Jasper is getting used to all the veggies."

Jasper put on what he thought was his best smile. "Sure. I love veggies."

He grunted when she elbowed him in the gut.

"Liar." She smiled.

"Caught me."

"That's why I also made lamb, so shut it. Both of you."

She glided back to the kitchen and Jasper watched her walk. He loved to watch those hips sway from side to side.

"Dude, you're drooling," Adam teased.

"Damn straight."

AFTER DINNER they laid on the couch, Willow snug in Jasper's arms and Adam on the other end, his feet on the table.

"I want to watch a movie. One we all like."

Jasper smiled. The three of them never could decide on one, and Willow usually got to pick whatever suited her fancy.

Yep, still love her. Every bit of her.

"Okay," Adam said. "Which one?"

"*Grease*?" Jasper asked.

Adam smacked him upside the head. "Dude, what is your fixation with that movie?"

He rubbed the back of his head. "Hey, that hurt. And I like Bad Sandy."

All three of them laughed at his odd choice for a movie.

"Really?" Willow asked once they could breathe again. "I could wear the leather pants if you want?"

Jasper groaned.

"Hey, not now. Not here." Adam waved his hands. "Let me watch the movie first. Then you two can go play 'You're the one that I want' with blindfolds and leather pants. But leave me out of it."

Jasper hugged them both close to him and laughed.

Oh, how he loved his family.

IT WAS funny how two little pink lines could cause a brain aneurism.

Okay, maybe not that as bad as that. But it could still change a person's life dramatically.

Oh, hell.

Willow was pregnant.

How did that happen?

She blushed when she thought about just exactly how that happened. Yeah, no condoms and mate marking proved fertile. Just ask Pat or Mel. Or now her.

She'd just gotten used to the whole werewolf thing. And that came after the whole being Jasper's mate thing. How was she supposed to be a mom on top of that?

Her head throbbed as the idea of sudden responsibility threatened to choke her. What if the Centrals wanted her baby? Her breaths came in pants as she began to hyper-ventilate.

Jasper knocked at the door, his sandalwood scent partially masked by worry.

"Willow, baby, what's wrong? I can feel your unease from the other side of the house."

She took a deep breath and tried to calm herself. Tried to tell him she was okay. But no words came out. Okay, apparently she wasn't okay. Her vision blackened. Okay, she *really* wasn't.

"Willow? I'm coming in."

A nod was her only response, though he couldn't see it through the closed, unlocked door. What was the point of locking a door in a house with a werewolf. They could get in anywhere they wanted. And apparently their sperm could do the same thing. Her poor unsuspecting egg. Why did the sex have to be so good?

Jasper walked into their master bath and took one look at her huddled on the ground. He switched his gaze to stare at the stick in her hand.

"Are we?" His voice cracked.

She could only nod. Like a dam bursting, tears flooded eyes and overfilled her eyes, spilling onto her cheeks.

Was he happy? Was she? Wasn't she supposed to be?

Damn it. She hated the fact that she feared the Centrals so much that they were ruining this for her.

Jasper stood still, his face expressionless.

Tears continued their trail down her face, soaking her shirt.

Her mate's face cracked in a huge smile. "A baby? Us?"

She nodded again. Okay, seriously? Why couldn't she speak?

Jasper walked toward her, studying her face, and his smile vanished.

"Wait, what's wrong. Are you sick? Is something wrong with the baby?" He pulled her in to his arms, hugging her, then pushed her back. "Wait, is that bad? Should I not touch you? I need to call North. Or Mom. Or the elders. Yeah. They'll know what to do."

His innocent and clearly panicked expression, along with his practically incoherent ramblings, washed away her own craziness. She let out a relived laugh.

"No, I'm fine. Really. No need to call in the cavalry. But you can call them over to tell them our news, later, if you want." She kissed him softly, and he relaxed against her.

"Willow, then, what was wrong? Why did you look so sad at the thought of being pregnant? I thought for a minute you didn't want it. I know it was fast, but it's okay. *I'm* happy."

She shook her head. "I was just worried. I'm sorry I freaked out."

Jasper angled his head. "You're allowed to freak out. I think it comes with the hormones. But, baby, wolves have babies all the time. Is it the shifting? Look at Mel, she shifts while she's pregnant. It's natural."

Willow nodded. She already knew about the shifting

and pregnancy. That wasn't new, but having it confirmed still came as a relief.

"But what about the Centrals?" There she'd said it. Voiced her concerns.

He let out a growl.

"Never again, Willow. I won't let them hurt you." He put his hand on her still-flat stomach, cradling her. "Or our baby."

Though she desperately wanted to believe him, she still had a lingering ounce of doubt. They'd taken her before. Broken the Redwoods' wards and trespassed on their lands. The Redwoods might be powerful, but the true evil the Centrals possessed crossed boundaries good couldn't and wouldn't cross. Would Hector and his Pack do it again? Take her or her child?

Willow put her hand over Jasper's. "I hope so."

She leaned into his hold, sitting on the bathroom floor, and vowed she wasn't weak anymore. No one would harm her child. And if they tried, she'd kill them. Slowly.

Yes, it was good to be a werewolf.

A WOMAN's scream filled the room. The hairs on the back of Jasper's neck rose and he cursed.

Dear God, what the hell is going on in there?

Jasper watched as Kade paced the room, waiting for Mel to give birth. She'd gone into labor in the middle of the night, and ten hours later, she was just now getting to the pushing.

How on Earth did women do it?

They'd sent most of the family home due to responsibilities and necessity of sleep, so Jasper was left alone with the soon-to-be-father, who currently was pacing a hole into the carpet.

"Why do I have to be out here?" Kade growled, pulling at his hair. "My mate is hurting in there. And I am stuck out here like a pup in the dog house. What did I do?"

Jasper laughed then felt a bit ill at the thought of Willow going through the same thing.

"Kade, you were just in there, remember? But Cailin threw you out."

Kade snarled. "Well, she's just the baby. What does she know? She had no right to do that."

"Dude, you were yelling at North to give her drugs, though you know wolves can't have them. I know she was in pain, but she was getting through it. You were the one freaking out. You threatened anyone who came near her. Cailin had every right to do what she did."

"Mel wanted me there. She needs me," Kade whined.

Poor guy. It must be brutal to know your mate is on the other side of the door in pain, but couldn't do a damn thing about it. Jasper did his best not to think of Willow lying on the bed, screaming in pain in just a few short months. At least one of the two of them in this room had to be sane.

"Mel was just being nice, Kade. In fact, I'm surprised she didn't kick your ass."

Kade blushed and stopped pacing. "Well…"

Jasper laughed. "Yes?"

"She might have threatened me with various acids that could dissolve bones and hide the bodies."

Jasper laughed, his side aching. Damn, he loved the chemist side of his sister-in-law.

Kade joined in his laughter. "But that may not have been because I was—as Cailin accused—hovering. It might have been because she blames me for putting her there."

Jasper sobered. "She'll be okay, Kade. Stop worrying. Women have been doing this for thousands of years."

Kade gave a bitter laugh. "Sure, remind me to say that when Willow is in this situation in about seven months."

Jasper shuddered. "Don't get me wrong, I am so happy that we're having a baby. But the whole pain thing is just too much. I don't know how they do it."

The sound of a baby crying froze both men in their tracks.

"That's why," Jasper rasped. "That's why they do it"

Their mother opened the door, a huge smile on her face and tears in her eyes. "Come on, Kade, come inside and meet your son."

"Finn," Kade whispered.

Pat nodded. "That is what Melanie said. Thank you so much for making me a grandmother."

She kissed him and gave him a fierce hug. Kade's cheeks were drenched with tears, and he walked through the door with a dazed expression on his face. Willow passed the new father on his way in.

She, too, was crying, and Jasper opened his arms. She slid against his side, and he hugged her close, inhaling her cinnamon scent.

Willow took a deep breath and sniffed. "We need to tell your father and brothers. I know Mel didn't want everyone here when they had duties, but they need to know."

Jasper kissed the top of her head. "We will, don't rush. Just let me hold you for a sec." He had an image of himself holding his son or daughter to his chest, and his body filled with warmth. He couldn't wait. It was something worth fighting for.

WILLOW WIPED down the remaining flour on the counter from the last batch of cinnamon rolls. She laughed at the familiar sensation. She'd been doing the same thing at a different bakery, but now things were so different. She wasn't alone anymore. She had a growing family. She did what she loved and was with a man she loved even more. And together they'd created a new life. A baby.

Something bad had to happen soon, right? Isn't that how it always happened?

She shook off that depressing thought. No use concentrating on something that might never come to pass.

Willow took out the now cooled sugar cookies from the shelf and started to frost them. She laughed at the little bunnies and deer forms. Wolves sure loved them in any form. The fact that it didn't bother her told her maybe she was starting to get a complex. She shrugged. Poor Bambi and Thumper.

Oh well, they tasted delicious, both in sugar and on the bone.

The bell rang over the door, but she didn't look around to see who it was right away. Reed was watching outside, and she knew it was safe. But the overwhelming potpourri scent invaded her nose, making her want to puke.

Camille.

"Well, Willow. It's nice to see you've gotten everything you deserve."

Her throaty voice set Willow's teeth on edge and made her want to throw something. Preferably something sharp and pointy. With poison.

Willow set her piping tube down and smiled.

"Camille, it's so nice to see you."

Right. Maybe in a vat of hot oil. Yes, that would be a nice way to see her.

Camille smiled, resembling a viper with sharp teeth.

"I just came here to show my support and tell you there are no hard feelings, despite what you may hear about me.

I'm so happy everything worked out with you and Jasper, your wolf...your baby. I hope you'll call me if you ever need help with...it."

Willow's stomach clenched at the thought of that smile and what lay behind it. Like hell that woman would go anywhere near her unborn child. She forced herself not to put a hand on her belly, protecting her young. She wouldn't show weakness.

"Thank you." She spoke though gritted teeth.

That woman was a bitch. A menace. She spent her time trailing behind the Jamenson men, trying to find a mate. Nipping on whatever bits of scraps people left for her. And these days, it seemed that Fredrick was the only one leaving anything around for her.

Camille sighed. "I just came into see if anything caught my fancy. But I don't see anything that suits my taste. You know how it is."

Bitch. Stuck up eats-too-many-sweets-as-it-is, bitch.

Willow raised a brow. "Well then, I'm sure you know the way out."

Damn, she really loved this new wolfy fierce side of hers.

Anger flashed over Camille's face, but the woman wouldn't get what she wanted. No, Willow wouldn't reach across the counter and smack a bitch.

Camille nodded then walked out the open door. She stopped once she reached the outside and glanced over her shoulder. Pain shot through Willow's head and Camille was gone.

Flashes of hands, a deep voice mingling with a higher one.

Willow gasped.

It was them.

Fredrick and Camille.

Oh my God.

They were the ones who'd kidnapped her and given her to the Centrals like a sack of flour to be traded. They were the traitors. Bile rose in Willow's throat. How could they go against the Pack? Hurt them like that?

Willow dropped the towel from her hand and ran.

Reed grabbed her arm and pulled her close as she made it out the door. She'd forgotten she wasn't alone, that her brother-in-law was there to protect her.

"Wait. Willow, what's wrong? What did Camille do?" Reed demanded.

"It was them..." She choked, too angry to cry.

"What? Who? Who was them? Tell me what's wrong."

She took a deep breath, trying to clear her thoughts. "I remember now. That night. The night with the dead girl. It was Camille and Fredrick. They took me. They helped the Centrals."

Reed's face turned to stone. He didn't ask how or why she suddenly knew but took out his phone and called Jasper.

Willow mentally slapped herself.

Why didn't she think to call? Her brain was too jumbled.

She heard Jasper growl and shout at the news.

Reed closed the phone and tugged on her arm. "Come on. Let's get you home. Jasper's waiting."

A howl split the air, followed by dozens more.

Slick oily magic filled the air, choking her.

Reed cursed. "We're under attack."

She was too late. She'd remembered too late. Camille and Fredrick had betrayed the Pack. Again. She only prayed she hadn't realized too late to save her family, her Pack, her home.

22

Jasper bent to pick up the phone he'd thrown against the wall in anger. He'd always known Camille was a slimy bitch and Fredrick a dumbass goon, but he'd never thought they would stoop to the level of betraying the Pack. Shouldn't he have felt something? Noticed something? Shouldn't Maddox have felt their cruelty through their emotions?

He shook his head. There was no use thinking about the what-ifs and whys. They'd fucked up. They'd let parasites, leeches, into their home, their Den, and his mate suffered for it. Jasper swallowed the lump of guilt in his throat. They'd kidnapped her. Stuck her with a needle and threw her at the feet of the depraved and soulless Centrals. They'd cut her, stripped her of her dignity, and forced him to bite and tear her flesh to make her a wolf.

Not all the Centrals though. There was one. The girl who'd helped Willow with that herb concoction. He would be forever grateful to whoever that was, for she'd saved his mate's life. But now Jasper would have to take a life, or give the responsibility to one in his family. Fredrick and Camille had to die. They needed to pay for their crimes and their sins.

He only hoped it hurt like hell.

A howl in the not too far distance stopped Jasper in his tracks.

What the hell?

A dozen more followed.

Dear God. We're under attack.

Heart pounding in his chest, he quickly dialed Adam. As the Enforcer, Adam would have information.

"What the hell is going on?" Jasper demanded.

"Our Den has been breached. The Centrals are coming!" Adam yelled.

Jasper could hear growling and fighting over the line. *Shit.*

"Jasper, they killed the sentries."

Fuck.

"Dammit, it won't end there." A howl again, this time closer to his home and familiar. "Did you hear that?"

"Yeah, it's Maddox. He's getting the families to the bunkers. I have Mom, Cailin, Mel, and Finn. And Dad is out protecting our people, along with the rest of the enforcers and our brothers."

"Good, we've prepared for this. Protect the weaker, kill the invaders. We can do it."

"Jasper, they knew exactly how to get past our shields. We've been betrayed."

He let out a painful breath. "Willow remembered. Camille and Fredrick. They're working with the Centrals."

Adam cursed. "Get out there. I'll take the circle; you get to the south side." His brother sighed. "Jasper, school was in session. I don't know if they got all the kids out or not."

"I'll check. I'll get everyone to safety."

"Take care of yourself."

"You too." They both hung up.

Jasper tucked the phone in his pocket and ran out the door. Damn it, he wanted to get to Willow. To make sure she was safe and inhale that sweet cinnamon scent. They were a pair, connected. He needed her and the child she carried more than breath. But Reed was with her. His little brother was strong and could protect her. And if he were honest with himself, Willow could take care of herself. That didn't mean she had to.

He jumped off the steps, his feet hitting the pavement of the sidewalk, and ran toward the howls. His Pack was in trouble, and he intended to save them – and kick the Central's ass. Though he didn't have proof it was them yet, there was no doubt in his mind who would be ballsy enough to encroach on their turf.

The Centrals would pay for what they've done.

He ran into the forest and the trees reached out and scratched his face, but he didn't care, his sole intent to find anyone who needed his help. In the distance, he saw a fallen man. He inhaled, catching the scent. Dammit, he was a Redwood. Jasper ran to the lifeless form and searched for a pulse.

There wasn't one.

A scream of fury ripped from his throat. Another life wasted because the bastards wanted power they didn't have the right or the soul to possess. His wolf rose to the surface, trying to take over, but Jasper set his teeth and remained in control. Though he wanted to go on a rampage and kill anything that crossed his path, it would do no good if he hurt someone he knew and cared about.

Another scent drifted on the breeze.

A Central.

And either an arrogant bastard who didn't care he was standing upwind or a fucking idiot. Jasper didn't care. He'd kill the fuckwit and show who actually held the power and strength.

"Change. You can take him as a wolf. Easy."

Jasper shook his head. No, he needed to be on two feet and totally in control. He needed to feel the pulse of the enemy fade beneath his fingertips. And for more practical reasons, he needed to be able to answer the phone in case someone called him for help – like Willow. It was hard to do that with paws, and despite what some people thought, werewolves were not telepathic.

Jasper crouched behind a tree, waiting for the ignorant fucker to walk his way. The brute of a man walked heavy-footed through the brush, not caring who heard him.

How much of an idiot was this guy?

Jasper inhaled again, trying to determine if the man might be leading him into a trap. No, the guy was alone. And a moron. He almost felt bad for the guy.

Within a breath, Jasper's arm shot out, and he twisted the Central's neck with a calming snapping sound. The other wolf lay dead at his feet, and he shook his head. Too easy. But worth it. He never liked killing for the sake of killing, but those who dared come on his land deserved what they got.

Jasper left both of the dead men where they lay. He would come back and deal with the bodies when he could. No matter which side, no one deserved to rot on the ground. Each deserved a proper burial. He ran through the forest, getting closer to the southern end where a large population lived, as well as where the school was. It chilled his blood to think of what he might come upon, but he continued on.

A group of five young wolves in their animal forms – not Redwoods – came out of the bushes, anger and an unhealthy glee in their eyes. Five on one, not great odds, but doable. The largest one jumped, teeth bared, and attacked. Jasper held out an arm and ducked, ripping the wolf by the scruff as he pivoted. The wolf yelped and tried to turn and bite, but Jasper growled and snapped its neck. He threw it at the four remaining wolves and snarled.

Two of them started forward and aimed at his legs.

Cheap bastards.

He faked left, then rolled to the right, letting the wolves run past then come back for him. He grabbed the knife from his boot and dug into both of their flanks, one right after the other. They collapsed onto each other, and Jasper finished them quickly. There were only a few Centrals he actually wanted to see suffer these nameless faces were not them. The last two wolves, seeing their compatriots fall, growled but did not attack him. Jasper growled back and rushed them. The wolves jumped, and Jasper grabbed them both, throwing them into a tree. He heard the distinct sound of bones breaking, but didn't know the damage. He raced to them both and killed them quickly.

Panting and tired, he wiped his knives on his jeans and left the the bodies behind. It took a lot of energy to fight like that in human form, but he was Beta; he could do it. But he needed to find his Pack and find out what exactly was going on. He needed to find Willow. Now.

He finally made it to the southern end and stopped, his mouth dropping. Utter devastation. Homes and businesses burned. People screaming. Children crying. What had the

Centrals done? And why didn't the Redwoods have the power to stop it?

Jasper continued toward the melee, fisting his hands. The smoke from the fires stung his nose and his anger increased. Why would they do this? What possible reason was there to kill women and children?

A small cry from behind a bench made Jasper freeze.

"Hey," Jasper whispered, using his most calm, soothing voice. "Come out. I'm safe. Smell me. I'm Jasper, the Beta. I'll get you where you need to be."

A small girl, around the age of five crawled out. Jasper picked her up and she snuggled under his chin, crying.

"Shh, darling. Come on. Let's get you to a safe house. Okay?" As Jasper wiped away some of the smudges on her cheeks, he finally recognized her. Larissa and Neil's oldest daughter. He tried not to think about what it meant that she was out here alone. And not with her parents, Kade and Melanie's best friends. "Gina, it's okay. I'll get you home."

At the mention of her name, she relaxed and stopped crying. "Okay, Mr. Jasper."

Jasper held her closer and ran to Larissa and Neil's home, praying someone was there.

"Gina!" Larissa ran out the door, hunting blade in hand, toward her daughter.

"Mommy!" Gina wiggled down from Jasper and jumped into her mother's arms. Larissa caught her with one hand, the other still carrying the blade, protecting them both.

Nothing like seeing a witch mother and werewolf mate in action.

"Jasper, thank God. I couldn't get to the school. I have the neighbors in our basement, and I'm setting wards. I can still feel Neil, and he called a while ago saying he's with your father. Thank you so much."

"It's no problem; get inside and be safe."

Larissa smiled and kissed Jasper's cheek. "You too. Kill them."

"Yes, ma'am."

Jasper ran off and helped others along the road find protection, fighting off invading wolves as he did. Where were all these guys coming from? And where the hell was Willow?

MORE SCREAMS REACHED Willow's ears, and she held tighter to Reed's hand. Though they had planned to run to her home and stash her there, she couldn't stomach leaving so many people in danger. Together, she and Reed had gotten most of the weaker wolves around them to safety and were herding the rest of them to a bunker. Thank God the Redwoods had plans for so many types of emergencies, because, in all the commotion, she wasn't sure she'd be able to do it herself.

"Willow, we need to go. Jasper will kill me if anything

happens to you or the baby. And frankly I like you too." Reed gave a nervous smile and pulled her down the road.

As they reached a corner, four wolves sprang out of the bushes. She inhaled, and that sickly oil scent invaded her nose.

Centrals.

Reed quickly went to work on the closest three, dodging blows and giving some of his own. But the last wolf only had eyes for her. She set her feet and braced for the wolf to launch. Adam and Jasper were teaching her self-defense, and she was stronger by far than when she was a human, but she was still learning and not nearly as good as Reed. The wolf growled and tried to bite her. She pivoted and kicked it in the face with all her strength. It collapsed at her feet, but was still breathing.

Reed came back from the three dead wolves – *go Reed* – and finished the last one for her.

"You shouldn't have to kill if you don't want to," Reed growled.

Relief coursed through her, and they ran toward her home. Where was Jasper? She needed him. Not to protect her, per se, but to be by her side. To know he was safe and away from Corbin and Camille. She held her stomach, her palm resting were her child lay, and prayed that Jasper would be safe.

A rustling of trees, a putrid scent, and a wolf jumped out of nowhere. Pain seared her arm, as sharp teeth nipped at her flesh. She growled and swiped at the wolf, anger making her wolf come to the surface. Reed snapped the other wolf's neck and kicked it for good measure.

"Shit, Willow. I couldn't smell that one coming until you did. There's too much in the air, too much magic, it's hindering my senses. Fuck. Are you okay? Let me see. How bad is it?" Reed was worried.

Willow took a deep breath. "I'm fine. It's not deep. Let's get out of here." She struggled to contain her wolf, who wanted to go out and kill something. But the human in her wasn't ready for that.

"Little Willow is bleeding again. How ironic."

A voice from the darkness caused the hair on the back of her neck to rise and nausea to roll in her stomach.

The demon walked toward them, a cruel smile on his lips.

Her heart stopped. He was faster than them. Stronger in all magic. What could she and Reed do?

"Willow." Reed smiled a sad smile. "Run."

The demon tilted his head and laughed. "One will do. Run away, little Willow. Go to your mate. Well, that is, if there is anything left of him after Camille is through with him."

No. He was lying. He had to be. That's what demons did. Jasper was fine. Right?

"Willow. Go."

"No, Reed." Tears fell. Between the stress and her hormones, she couldn't hold them back.

"Find Jasper. I'll be fine." The look on Reed's face told her he didn't believe that any more than she did.

Reed pushed her, and she ran. Ran to her mate and away from her brother by marriage. She'd be back. She'd get Jasper, and they'd save Reed. That was what was going to happen. He wouldn't fall. No. He'd be fine, just like he said.

She ran into the forest, and though she'd past her line of vision. She was still close enough to hear the demon's laugh and Reed's pain filled scream.

Close enough for the scent of Reed's blood to reach her nose.

Willow opened her mouth and screamed for help. For Jasper. For anyone. Just for someone to come with the strength to make this go away and take vengeance. To save Reed – if there was anything left to save.

23

Willow's scream for help reached Jasper's ears, and his body twitched with horror. Was she hurt? He ran toward her screams, praying he wouldn't find her help-less and in pain. He cleared a fallen log and came up behind her.

"Willow!"

"Oh, Jasper."

She jumped into his embrace, her tears soaking his shirt. He squeezed her hard, making sure she was real and not a dream. She crushed her mouth to his, kissing him with all her might. He inhaled her scent, grateful for the sweet cinnamon smell, until he smelled the tangy scent of blood lingering beneath.

"You're hurt," he rasped.

"I'm fine. Really. It's just a scrape."

Jasper shook his head. "No, you're bleeding."

"I'm fine. I'll heal. But Jasper," she choked out. "I think they killed Reed."

He froze. "What? What did you say?"

"The demon. He killed him. Or at least hurt him badly. The demon came for us and Reed told me to run. I didn't want to, Jasper. I almost didn't." She took a deep breath. "But the demon said you were in trouble, but you aren't." She choked up again and shook her head.

"Breathe, baby. Tell me what happened."

"I left. I left him there. I ran to come for you. Reed pushed me away. And then I heard the demon laugh and Reed scream. That's when I called for help and ran back to him. I couldn't let Reed die like that. But he wasn't there, Jasper. He's gone."

Willow broke down, and he held her close.

Jesus. Reed. His baby brother. Gone? Had the demon killed him? Or just taken him? And if he did, why? Jasper shuddered. And if the bastard took his brother, what would he do to him? Would Reed even want to live after something like that?

"Willow, it's not your fault. You did the right thing. You protected our baby. Reed can take care of himself. I'm sure he's okay." Even to his own ears, it sounded like a lie. But he didn't like the alternative. It wasn't an option.

"Jasper, what about the Pack? The children? Is everyone safe?"

"I know most are but not all. But we need to get out of the forest and find the others. I don't think we lost too many, but losing just one is one too many." Jasper clenched his teeth as rage fought with the sorrow inside him.

"We lost some? Who?"

"I don't know, baby."

He went stone cold. He wouldn't cry because it wouldn't accomplish anything, but he held Willow close. The pain at losing so many at the hands of evil felt as though it would crush him, but he couldn't let it. He had to be strong for Willow, for his Pack.

Someone stepped on a branch behind him, and he went on alert, covering Willow. Jasper inhaled and growled at the intruder. The soon to be dead intruder.

Fredrick.

"Took you long enough to remember, bitch. But it's okay. Your Pack will die soon, and I will be in the power at the side of greatness, rather than below the feet of you shits." Fredrick growled.

"How could you to that to your Pack? You were part of us? How could you betray us?" Jasper asked.

"Easy, you are nothing. Worth nothing."

Jasper shook his head. All this for power? For not being part of the Jamensons? Pack hierarchy was blood, driven by instinct, not by choice. Fredrick had been born low on the totem pole but not looked down upon because of it. As a pup, they'd cherished him because he was a gift – like all children. But as a man, he was barely tolerated but because of his attitude, not because of his low status in the Pack.

The betrayal to the Pack alone warranted the other man's death. But because he'd a hand in hurting Willow, no, Fredrick would die by his hand. Now.

Fredrick pulled out a knife and lunged. Jasper pushed Willow to the ground and she crawled for cover under a log, protecting her stomach. Jasper ducked under the blade and rammed his shoulder into the other man's gut. Fredrick grunted and bent over, dropping the blade. *Damned stupid werewolf.*

Jasper elbowed the man in the jaw, forcing Fredrick to the ground. Jasper straddled him, dropping his own knife, and pummeled the other man's face and chest with his fists. He shouted and took out his rage for the loss of Reed, hurting Willow, the dead wolf in the forest, Gina's tears. Everything. He pounded and pounded until his fists were bloodied.

"Jasper, stop. He's dead. Baby. Stop." Willow brushed his arm with her fingers.

He dropped his hands and rested his face on her stomach, inhaling her scent. The bastard was dead by his own hands, but he didn't feel any better. Didn't know if he ever would.

"Wow. So barbaric." They turned toward the sound of the voice Camille laughed and clapped, starting the pair. "Wait until you meet my little demon friend."

Jasper growled and lifted off the dead man, preparing to leap at the bitch and kill. But before he could launch himself toward the woman who tried to ruin his life, Jasper flew through the air, Willow right beside him. An unseen force threw them across the path to the ground. He grunted on impact and reached out for Willow.

What the hell?

He pulled her close and covered her with his body, praying that she and the baby were okay.

Jasper heard laughter, and the previously unseen force stepped from the trees.

"Oh, you can't protect your mate for too long. But go on trying. It amuses me," the demon crooned.

"You should have picked me, Jasper," Camille said. "I would have been better than the trash you are laying on." She pulled a gun from behind her back, raised it, and pulled the trigger.

Hot, searing pain burst through his arm, but nowhere else. It hurt like hell, but could have been worse. He did his best to cover Willow more.

"Jasper, you're hurt," she whispered.

"I'm okay."

Camille laughed again. "Not for long. I'm going with my Corbin. A man with real power, not someone who begs for his daddy's love."

Jasper pulled on his Beta powers and took a deep breath. "Camille. You are cut off. Pack no more. Shunned."

He could feel the tendril of connection snap, and the last of his energy leave him. It took considerable power to cut off a Pack member. It usually took the Alpha or Heir to do it, but Jasper was just strong enough to pull it off.

Camille screamed in pain, writhing on the ground. The demon sighed, lifted her, and threw her over his shoulder, fading from sight as he was a ghost.

Another howl split the air. This time a Redwood. The Centrals were retreating. For now.

He sat up and pulled Willow with him. "Come on. Let's go see the mess and try to figure out what we are going to do.

Willow kissed him softly, somehow making his hurts fade away. "I love you."

"I love you, too."

REED WAS GONE. Not even a blood trail. Willow could only guess that the demon had taken him the same way he did Camille. She prayed he was still alive. He had to be. What would her new family do if they lost him? Willow shuddered to think.

It was all her fault. Reed was gone, possibly dead, because he'd sacrificed himself for her.

Jasper kissed her softly. "Stop thinking what you're thinking."

"You don't read minds." But he always seemed to know anyway.

"I don't need to. Your thoughts are all over your face." He held her close. She inhaled his scent and calmed. "Baby, whatever happened to Reed, it wasn't your fault."

She took an achy breath. "It sure feels that way."

She sank into his hold, taking whatever comfort she could. At least they were alive. She felt horrible even thinking it, but in the grand scheme of things, Jasper was her rock. Without him, she'd break.

Willow looked around the block, the faint smell of ash and fire tickling her nose. Buildings were ruined, crumbling to the ground. Children were crying, clinging onto their mothers. It looked like a war zone.

Her heart clenched, sorrow sweeping over her.

It *was* a war zone.

North and Pat had set up a triage station in front of her bakery. Most of the wounds were small, and those that weren't would heal relatively fast because of their werewolf abilities. The children would take a bit longer to heal, but all of them were wolves. But some people were witches. They would heal faster than humans but were still more fragile than a werewolf.

"Momma? Daddy?" A young girl around three toddled over the broken path, unhurt but crying.

Where were her mother and father?

Willow ran to her and enveloped the girl in her arms.

The girl wrapped her arms around Willow's neck and held on for dear life.

"Shh, it's okay. What's your name, hon?" Willow held her close, feeling the little girl's heart beat slow against her. At least she was calming down. It felt good to be the one to offer comfort.

"Emily." She rasped. "Momma? Daddy?"

Willow looked over Emily's head toward Jasper, who knew the list of casualties. He shook his head, pain in his eyes. Willow's heart broke. Oh, poor Emily.

A single tear fell down her cheek. She didn't have much left as it was. The injustice of it all was too much to take. *Was it worth it, Centrals? All of this death and destruction?* Was whatever power they thought they held worth Emily's pain? To know that in the morning when she woke, her mom and dad wouldn't be there. They wouldn't watch her grow up, finish school, get a job, get married. They would miss all the moments in Emily's life because of the greediness of a Pack. Was it worth it?

She wanted to yell all this. Scream and shout. But what would it accomplish besides scare the little girl crying in her arms, begging for her momma and daddy. Her momma and daddy who wouldn't answer her. They had to fight against this evil. Crush it. She couldn't let another fate like Emily's come to pass.

"Emily!"

A woman ran toward Willow and Emily, tears running

down her face, arms outstretched.

"Aunt Beth!" Emily screamed and wiggled out of Willow's hold. The girl ran toward her aunt, and Beth took her in her arms.

Relief, however little it might be, spread though her. Emily wasn't alone in the world. But it still didn't make the loss hurt any less.

Twenty-six. They'd lost twenty-six wolves. They'd also killed over forty enemy wolves. But that retribution didn't make it any better.

"Thank you. Thank you for finding her," Beth said.

Willow nodded.

The other woman's eyes held pain and recognition. She knew her sister or brother wouldn't be coming for Emily, that her life was now forever changed as Emily became her responsibility.

Beth squared her shoulders, nodded once, and carried Emily off, leaving Willow standing alone on the corner, not knowing what to do next. She rested her palm on her belly, cradling her child. Would this little one's fate be the same as Emily's?

Sandalwood enveloped her as Jasper wrapped his arms around her waist, placing his hand over hers, over their child.

"We will find Reed, Willow. We will have our vengeance. For Emily and everyone else who lost someone today," Jasper vowed, his breath ticking her ear.

Willow shook her head.

"But at what cost, Jasper? Will it be enough? Vengeance won't bring those people back. Vengeance won't help us find Reed. But stopping them will. Stopping the Centrals from doing worse. That will bring something back, something lost."

Jasper nodded and held her closer. She leaned back into her mate and closed her eyes. Would it be enough? Was she strong enough?

"Jasper, you can't come with me," Adam grumbled.

Jasper clenched his fists and tried not to hit his own brother. They'd left the town square and reconvened at his parents' house to discuss what they would do about patrols, funerals, family, and Reed. His body ached from the fighting, his strength depleted and his heart heavy from loss, but right now, he fed on his anger.

"You want to go alone to find Reed?" Jasper asked.

"No, I don't *want* to go alone. But what other choice do I have?" Adam growled.

"Then I'll go with you."

"And what? Leave the family alone? Leave your pregnant wife to fend for herself?" Adam retorted.

"Kade, North, and Maddox are here."

"And it will take all of you and more to rebuild our

home while protecting it. And you can't leave Willow. You know that."

Jasper sighed. Dammed wolf was right. That didn't mean he had to like it.

"I don't like you going off alone," Jasper grumbled.

"It needs to be done. There is magic blocking Reed's location. We don't know where they took him, so I'll need to search. Alone, I can be more secretive. But we can still feel Reed, Jasper. We know he's alive."

Thank God.

Jasper exhaled and nodded. "Find our brother Adam. We can't lose him."

A solemn look passed over Adam's face. He must be thinking about Anna and the baby. They were too late that time, but they couldn't be again. They wouldn't survive if they were.

Jesus, his family had been through too much already.

Jasper pulled Adam into a hug and held him close. Going on the Central's land would be no walk in the park. There was a good chance he'd lose both of his brothers in this debacle, but he couldn't think about that.

He released Adam, and watched him walk out the door. He prayed this wouldn't be the last time he'd see him.

Please, let him bring home Reed. Alive.

Reed was the center of their family, the funny one who pulled them together. Without him, what would they do?

Jasper didn't want to find out.

24

———

Willow winced as Jasper washed out her cut with saline – again. They'd gotten home a half hour ago, and the man had cleaned her arm four times. Her arm was already healing due to her awesome werewolf powers. However, the adorable look of concentration on his face melted her heart.

"Jasper, it's clean. I'm fine. It's only a scratch. Really," she whispered and brushed away the lock that loved to fall out of place into his eyes.

Her mate exhaled and rested his forehead on her shoulder, rubbing circles on her wrist with the pad of his thumb. Tiny tingles of something warm and needy raced up her arm, wrapping around not just her heart but also her womb.

Jesus, she loved this man. Needed this man.

She ran her hand down his back and tucked her fingers under his shirt, loving the heat of his skin. He lifted his head and rubbed his nose on her cheek before he trailed kisses along her jawline, behind her ear, and to her lips. She opened her mouth, welcoming him. His tongue massaged hers, languid and slow.

Jasper pulled back and bit her lip. "Let's take a shower. I need to wash the day away."

They stood, and she lifted her arms. Waiting. Jasper leaned down and kissed her again, fisting his hands in the bottom of her shirt. After releasing her lips, he slowly pulled it over her head. He ran his palm down her stomach, hovering over her still flat belly, and unbuttoned her jeans. He crouched and peeled them from her legs, kissing the spot that held their child. She loved the way his whiskers scraped her skin.

She wiggled her hips, and he laughed.

"I love you, baby," Jasper whispered.

Willow sighed. "I love you, too."

He stripped off her panties and bra. Her breasts fell, aching, needy for his palms. He seemed to read her mind and cupped them, rubbing her nipples with the pads of his fingers.

Man, he had talented fingers. Whether it be his talent for wood working or his loving of her body, Jasper knew what to do with his hands. Lucky her.

"I thought you wanted a shower," she rasped.

Wait? Why am I stopping him?

Jasper laughed. "Yes, I did. But we can do both at the same time." He stood up and raised his hands like she had, causing her to giggle.

She stripped him of his shirt, pausing to caress his abs.

Seriously, who outside a romance novel has an eight pack?

He removed his pants and his boxer briefs in one move. Damn, she loved the way his cock sprang forth, tapping his stomach.

Yum.

Jasper took her hand and led her to the shower. He turned on the water to a warm, not-too-hot, not-too-cold temperature then stood in front of the spray, shielding her eyes.

Caring was her werewolf.

He turned, allowing the water to run down her body. It felt warm, refreshing after such a long day of heart-wrenching turmoil. She jumped when Jasper first touched her with his soapy hand. He used the soap on his palms to clean her body in slow, core-clenching circles. She returned the favor, washing away the dirt and blood from his battles.

Her warrior werewolf.

They rinsed themselves, and she wrapped her arms around his waist, his erection hard against her belly. He leaned down and captured her lips for a kiss, gently lifting her up against the wall. She wrapped her legs around his waist, and he slid inside. She gasped. So smooth and wet, no need for preparation.

The water beat down on his back and her arms as he stood there, savoring the moment She kissed him back, loving his taste, and he began to move. Slowly. Surely. They kept their eyes open, hardly blinking, their gazes connected. With each thrust, she felt his love, his determination to protect her. Water slid down their skin, pooling where they connected, trailing down his powerful legs that kept them both steady.

They came together in a slow rise of passion, their gazes never breaking. She watched as his pupils dilated, the green rim of color growing small under a rim of glowing gold as he came.

They stood there together, him still hard in her, until the water grew cold.

She yelped at the sudden temperature change.

"I guess we've been in here for a bit." He gave her a sheepish smile and pulled out, lowering her legs to the floor. He quickly turned off the water.

Willow reached out for a towel to dry him, but he took it from her with a shake of his head. He dried her with soft pats and kisses then dried himself.

God, she was so tired. Sore. Sad. But the love-making helped.

That is what your mate it for. To be there in times of need, to help you in any way he can.

Willow agreed with her wolf, loving the way Jasper cared for her.

Once dry, Jasper put the towel back on the rack and picked her up, cradled her to his chest.

"Ready for bed?" Jasper kissed the crown of her head, and she snuggled closer.

She nodded, and he carried her, naked, to bed.

He laid her down and covered her with the comforter, sliding in behind to spoon her.

"I wouldn't want you to get cold," he rumbled.

Willow sighed. "I like it." She wiggled her butt and felt his hardness against the crease. *Gotta love werewolf stamina.* "I'm tired but not." She laughed. "I think I'm going crazy."

Jasper nipped her earlobe, sending shivers down her spine. "Makes perfect sense to me."

Taking the initiative, she turned around and lifted to straddle his waist.

Jasper smiled a purely sinful smile. "Are you ready for me?"

"Always," she whispered.

She leaned down and kissed him, licking the seam of his lips and playing with his tongue. She lifted slightly, and he slid inside her core. She sat up and smiled, loving the feel of control from being on top, watching her all-too-masculine mate lying beneath her. Locking her feet under his thighs, she lifted up his length and fell back down again. He gripped her hips and she lifted up and down, over and over again, riding him. Her breasts bounced, and she laughed. A werewolf cowgirl in all her glory. He moved his hands, trailing up to take a breast in hand, the other rubbing circles around her clit. Again, they came together, his seed warming her from the inside out.

She lay on top of him, feeling his heartbeat beneath her cheek. Thank God he walked in the door of her bakery. Even through it all, she wouldn't change it. She had Jasper and the baby in her belly. They were worth all the pain and anguish. She had a family now.

Willow held Jasper closer. She'd never let go. He was hers. Now and forever.

JASPER SAT IN HIS PARENTS' house the next day, waiting for their dinner to begin. Willow sat beside him in his arms, his hand protectively on her stomach. She wasn't showing yet, but she would. He couldn't wait to see her grow round with his child. He might be Beta of the Redwoods, but he was Alpha in that respect.

He nuzzled her temple and kissed it softly. "Are you ready for the mating ceremony in a few days?"

She grinned. "Of course. Though it seems odd now to have one since I already have your last name and think of you as my husband and mate."

Pride filled him as he took her lips in a deep kiss. "We've

done all of this, I know, but I want to give you a day that's all yours."

"Ours," she countered.

"Ours." He pulled her closer and gazed around the room.

Cailin paced in front of the fireplace, anger pouring out of her in waves. But honestly, that always seemed to be the case lately. Maddox sat in his usual corner, close to his family, but not touching. His mother's cheeks held tear streaks, but she was strong. Steady. The wife of the Alpha had to be. And his mother was more Alpha than most of the men in the Pack. Mel stood and rocked baby Finn, keeping him quiet. Edward stood on the other side of the room with North and Kade, discussing how to better protect the Den. Jasper could hear what they had to say, and would speak up if needed, but he liked where he was, sitting with his mate.

This was his family. But not all of it. They weren't whole – not without Reed. Not without Adam.

His mother's quiet voice interrupted. "Dinner is ready."

As a group, they ventured to the dining room, eating their roast and mashed potatoes, but not tasting. They were werewolves, they needed the fuel and nutrients. But the absence of Reed and Adam was the elephant in the room. Their absence was the rip in their structure, creating a vacuum, sucking the warmth and joy of a family gathering.

The Centrals had come onto their land and tried to break them. And almost succeeded.

Once they got Reed back, they would be better. But the Centrals needed to pay – dearly.

Willow snuggled into his side. "I love you."

He bent down and kissed her. "I love you, too."

Jasper was so thankful he had walked into that bakery that day and scented her sweet cinnamon. He loved the way his mate tasted. He always would. He couldn't believe the steps they'd walked, but he was grateful for where they had lead. He had his Willow, his child to be. He had his growing family. He'd do anything to protect them.

They were his.

EPILOGUE

"Well, my Corbin, everything worked out," Camille purred next to him. "We broke them, and we have a Redwood prince. I call this a good day."

Corbin smiled and then slit her throat.

The pawn in his plan slid to the floor, her lifeless body heavy against his legs, her glassy eyes wide with shock.

But really, how could the bitch have been so surprised?

Corbin shook his head. No, Camille wasn't his mate. There was only one, but she was long gone. She'd left before he'd even made this plan, before he'd met Willow to play with. But that was neither here nor there.

His footsteps echoed as he walked through the dungeon, a smile on his face. His demon, Caym, walked behind him. Such a good expense, this demon. What was the life of two family members when he had a demon that could take his Pack and him to greater power?

His captive lay on the ground, shackled to the wall. Reed Jamenson. The Alpha's son.

Corbin shook his head. *Stupid wolf. Trying to save that bitch Willow. Was it worth it?*

Caym rubbed his shoulder. Comfort swelled. The demon was right. No use getting frustrated over the actions of cannon fodder. He'd kill the wolf soon. Fun.

The door opened behind him, and his father walked in.

"I see you've taken care of Camille. Good. She annoyed me. But have someone take care of the body. I'm not in the mood for the stench." Hector turned to Caym. "And good job capturing that wolf. The Jamensons might pay for him or at least put up a good fight. If they don't do anything about it, then Corbin has a plaything for a bit. No harm, no foul."

Excitement shot through him. Oh yes, that sounded like a plan.

The demon smiled coldly at them both. A shiver of evil and pain slid down his skin, arousing him.

Nice.

Reed lifted his head, and Corbin smiled.

"You will bring us greatness, Reed," his father said. "I hope it's through your death."

Reed just smiled with blood on his lips. "Bring it."

Anger coursed through him. *Fucking Redwood ego.*

A whimper sounded from the corner.

Ah, the witch.

"Watch what you say," Hector warned. "Or we'll hurt the girl. And enjoy it."

Reed stiffened and looked toward the witch, need evident on his face.

Interesting.

The Jamensons would know who they messed with. The stupid Jamensons would call for their lost son, and the Centrals would rule. With Caym by his side, he could do no wrong. They would win, and the world would bleed. And Corbin would rejoice.

The End

Next up in the Redwood Pack series: TRINITY BOUND

A NOTE FROM CARRIE ANN

Thank you so much for reading **A TASTE FOR A MATE!**

Next in the series?

Reed finds his mates in <u>Trinity Bound!</u>

If you want to make sure you know what's coming next from me, you can sign up for my newsletter at www. CarrieAnnRyan.com; follow me on twitter at @CarrieAnn-Ryan, or like my Facebook page. I also have a Facebook Fan Club where we have trivia, chats, and other goodies. You guys are the reason I get to do what I do and I thank you.

Make sure you're signed up for my MAILING LIST so you can know when the next releases are available as well as find giveaways and FREE READS.

Happy Reading!

Redwood Pack Series:

Book 1: <u>An Alpha's Path</u>

Book 2: <u>A Taste for a Mate</u>

Book 3: <u>Trinity Bound</u>

<u>Redwood Pack Box Set</u> (Contains Books 1-3)

Book 3.5: <u>A Night Away</u>

Book 4: <u>Enforcer's Redemption</u>

Book 4.5: <u>Blurred Expectations</u>

Book 4.7: <u>Forgiveness</u>

Book 5: <u>Shattered Emotions</u>

Book 6: <u>Hidden Destiny</u>

Book 6.5: <u>A Beta's Haven</u>

Book 7: <u>Fighting Fate</u>

Book 7.5: <u>Loving the Omega</u>

Book 7.7: <u>The Hunted Heart</u>

Book 8: <u>Wicked Wolf</u>

<u>The Complete Redwood Pack Box Set</u> (Contains Books 1-7.7)

Want to keep up to date with the next Carrie Ann Ryan
Release? Receive Text Alerts easily!

Text CARRIE to 24587

ABOUT THE AUTHOR

Carrie Ann Ryan is the New York Times and USA Today bestselling author of contemporary, paranormal, and young adult romance. Her works include the Montgomery Ink, Redwood Pack, Fractured Connections, and Elements of Five series, which have sold over 3.0 million books worldwide. She started writing while in graduate school for her advanced degree in chemistry and hasn't stopped since.

Carrie Ann has written over seventy-five novels and novellas with more in the works. When she's not losing herself in her emotional and action-packed worlds, she's reading as much as she can while wrangling her clowder of cats who have more followers than she does.

www.CarrieAnnRyan.com

ALSO FROM CARRIE ANN RYAN

The Montgomery Ink: Fort Collins Series:

Book 1: Inked Persuasion

Book 2: Inked Obsession

Book 3: Inked Devotion

Book 4: Inked Craving

The On My Own Series:

Book 1: My One Night

Book 2: My Rebound

Book 3: My Next Play

Book 4: My Bad Decisions

The Tattered Royals Series:

Book 1: Royal Line

Book 2: Enemy Heir

The Ravenwood Coven Series:

Book 1: Dawn Unearthed

Book 2: Dusk Unveiled

Book 3: Evernight Unleashed

Montgomery Ink:

Book 0.5: Ink Inspired

Book 0.6: Ink Reunited

Book 1: Delicate Ink

Book 1.5: Forever Ink

Book 2: Tempting Boundaries

Book 3: Harder than Words

Book 3.5: Finally Found You

Book 4: Written in Ink

Book 4.5: Hidden Ink

Book 5: Ink Enduring

Book 6: Ink Exposed

Book 6.5: Adoring Ink

Book 6.6: Love, Honor, & Ink

Book 7: Inked Expressions

Book 7.3: Dropout

Book 7.5: Executive Ink

Book 8: Inked Memories

Book 8.5: Inked Nights

Book 8.7: Second Chance Ink

Montgomery Ink: Colorado Springs

Book 1: Fallen Ink

Book 2: Restless Ink

Book 2.5: Ashes to Ink

Book 3: Jagged Ink

Book 3.5: Ink by Numbers

The Montgomery Ink: Boulder Series:

Book 1: Wrapped in Ink

Book 2: Sated in Ink

Book 3: Embraced in Ink

Book 4: Seduced in Ink

Book 4.5: Captured in Ink

The Gallagher Brothers Series:

Book 1: Love Restored

Book 2: Passion Restored

Book 3: Hope Restored

The Whiskey and Lies Series:

Book 1: Whiskey Secrets

Book 2: Whiskey Reveals

Book 3: Whiskey Undone

The Fractured Connections Series:

Book 1: Breaking Without You

Book 2: Shouldn't Have You

Book 3: Falling With You

Book 4: Taken With You

The Less Than Series:

Book 1: Breathless With Her

Book 2: Reckless With You

Book 3: Shameless With Him

The Promise Me Series:

Book 1: Forever Only Once

Book 2: From That Moment

Book 3: Far From Destined

Book 4: From Our First

Redwood Pack Series:

Book 1: An Alpha's Path

Book 2: A Taste for a Mate

Book 3: Trinity Bound

Book 3.5: A Night Away

Book 4: Enforcer's Redemption

Book 4.5: Blurred Expectations

Book 4.7: Forgiveness

Book 5: Shattered Emotions

Book 6: Hidden Destiny

Book 6.5: A Beta's Haven

Book 7: Fighting Fate

Book 7.5: Loving the Omega

Book 7.7: The Hunted Heart

Book 8: <u>Wicked Wolf</u>

The Talon Pack:

Book 1: <u>Tattered Loyalties</u>

Book 2: <u>An Alpha's Choice</u>

Book 3: <u>Mated in Mist</u>

Book 4: <u>Wolf Betrayed</u>

Book 5: <u>Fractured Silence</u>

Book 6: <u>Destiny Disgraced</u>

Book 7: <u>Eternal Mourning</u>

Book 8: <u>Strength Enduring</u>

Book 9: <u>Forever Broken</u>

The Elements of Five Series:

Book 1: From Breath and Ruin

Book 2: From Flame and Ash

Book 3: From Spirit and Binding

Book 4: From Shadow and Silence

The Branded Pack Series:

(Written with Alexandra Ivy)

Book 1: <u>Stolen and Forgiven</u>

Book 2: <u>Abandoned and Unseen</u>

Book 3: <u>Buried and Shadowed</u>

Dante's Circle Series:

Book 1: <u>Dust of My Wings</u>

Book 2: <u>Her Warriors' Three Wishes</u>

Book 3: <u>An Unlucky Moon</u>

Book 3.5: <u>His Choice</u>

Book 4: <u>Tangled Innocence</u>

Book 5: <u>Fierce Enchantment</u>

Book 6: <u>An Immortal's Song</u>

Book 7: <u>Prowled Darkness</u>

Book 8: Dante's Circle Reborn

Holiday, Montana Series:

Book 1: <u>Charmed Spirits</u>

Book 2: <u>Santa's Executive</u>

Book 3: <u>Finding Abigail</u>

Book 4: <u>Her Lucky Love</u>

Book 5: Dreams of Ivory

The Happy Ever After Series:

<u>Flame and Ink</u>

<u>Ink Ever After</u>

www.ingramcontent.com/pod-product-compliance
Lightning Source LLC
Chambersburg PA
CBHW061521210726
48287CB00006B/1771